Soul Tourists

Bernardine Evaristo

PENGUIN BOOKS

PENGUIN BOOKS

Published by the Penguin Group
Penguin Books Ltd, 80 Strand, London WC2R 0RL, England
Penguin Group (USA) Inc., 375 Hudson Street, New York, New York 10014, USA
Penguin Group (Canada), 90 Eglinton Avenue East, Suite 700, Toronto, Ontario, Canada M4P 2Y3
(a division of Pearson Penguin Canada Inc.)
Penguin Ireland, 25 St Stephen's Green, Dublin 2, Ireland
(a division of Penguin Books Ltd)
Penguin Group (Australia), 250 Camberwell Road, Camberwell, Victoria 3124, Australia
(a division of Pearson Australia Group Pty Ltd)
Penguin Books India Pvt Ltd, 11 Community Centre, Panchsheel Park, New Delhi – 110 017, India
Penguin Group (NZ), cnr Airborne and Rosedale Roads, Albany, Auckland 1310, New Zealand
(a division of Pearson New Zealand Ltd)
Penguin Books (South Africa) (Pty) Ltd, 24 Sturdee Avenue, Rosebank, Johannesburg 2196, South Africa

Penguin Books Ltd, Registered Offices: 80 Strand, London WC2R 0RL, England

www.penguin.com

First published by Hamish Hamilton 2005
Published in Penguin Books 2006
1

The publisher would like to thank A. P. Watt on behalf of the Royal Literary Fund
for permission to reproduce the extract from *The Poet and the Lunatic* by
G. K. Chesterton on p. vii

The moral right of the author has been asserted

Set in Minion
Designed by Nicky Barneby @ Barneby Ltd
Typeset by Rowland Phototypesetting Ltd, Bury St Edmunds, Suffolk
Printed in England by Clays Ltd, St Ives plc

ISBN-13: 978–0–140–29782–9
ISBN-10: 0–140–29782–0

For my mother, Jacqueline Mary Evaristo,
who is simply amazing

They say travel broadens the mind,
but you must have the mind.

G. K. Chesterton,
The Poet and the Lunatic

Contents

The Shipwreck, 1987   3

Heaven, Really   11

Flying to Tower Hamlets   14

The Coroner's Office   16

The Burial Ground   19

Single at Mingles, 1988   25

Café Italia, Soho   28

Broadstairs-sur-la-Mer   43

Clerken-well   57

Fifty-one Days in Blackheath   75

London Au Revoir   81

La France   84

The Freeway   85

Hall of Mirrors, Versailles   91

The Queen of France's Boudoir   98

A Caravan in a Country Lane   100

The Convent   104

Café des Fantômes, Paris   111

The Camargue   127

Morning in a French Lay-by   128

A Thousand Miles from Home   130

The Campsite   132

Summer on the Coast   135

The Crying Mountain   145

Seeing Red in Orange Square, Marbella   147

Rock of Jabal al-Tariq   153

The Room in Jessie's Head   161

Mama Hortense's Singing Kitchen   163

Closing Time at Mama's   168

The Alps   173

The Fêted House of Medici, Florence   185

Continental Shift, Turkey   195

The Silken Road   203

Letter from the Court of Jessie at Ölüdeniz   209

Summer of 1989: Court Budget   216

Dreams of a Faraway Place   218

A Trip Down Memory Lane   221

Old Istanbul   233

Eighteenth-century Slave Market   235

In the Sultan's Seraglio   241

Life after the Camp Deserter   247

The Front Line   251

Güle, Güle, Ölüdeniz   254

The Ocean Floor   256

Eastern Anatolia   261

Slipping into the Middle East   266

The Supreme Court of 'Justice'   273

Antipodean Dreamtime   277

The Glorious Gulf   281

Epilogue: Under the Carpet at Windsor   285

Acknowledgements   291

The Shipwreck, 1987

The Blackwall Tunnel is the birth canal forcing me underneath the pressurized gallons of the river that splits the city into north and south.

Every week I have to leave the Saturday-morning sky-view from my flat in the grand Georgian crescent of the Paragon, which faces the wide green flatland of Blackheath. The sky is the mother of all shape-shifters, but, whether tumultuous with rain and storms, washed out with cold or reflecting the brilliance of an imaginary blue, if I look long enough, I can attach my worries to an itinerant cloud and watch it drift away.

Every week, as I descend into the tunnel's arched, prowling depths, headlights dipped, windows closed because of the damned fumes, I dread the moment when I'm finally pushed out, noiselessly screaming, tiny fists clenched, eyes all screwed up and gummy, face blue and bruised like a little boxer, into the thundering traffic and toxic air of the Isle of Dogs, and from there, it's a short drive to the house where my father rots like a carcass of rancid beef.

I park outside the only house in the street visibly subsiding, switch off the engine and prepare in a moment's silence. It's like sitting on the ocean bed and looking out on to a long-forgotten shipwreck.

Sandwiched between identical one-storey terraces, all of which have gleaming windows and neatly pruned hedges, is my father's roof with its mosaic of ill-matched tiles. Quartered window-panes, frames black and fissured, are streaked with the greasy residue of the tar of cigarettes. A pile of bricks taken from the crumbling street wall is stuck in the middle of his garden, rising like a triumphant ruin out of weeds and tall grass. The path to the front door has missing slabs, and my way is blocked, as usual, by a tall green wheelie-bin, standing where the dustmen left it the week before.

I climb the three steps, which are cracked and sink at a right angle, ring the bell and look through the letter-box. The stench of warm urine hits my nostrils, but thankfully not the aroma of a dead body, which I suspect I would recognize.

I turn the key in the lock, and let myself in.

My father moved here twelve years ago, but the top floor hasn't been used at all and the ceilings are caving in. This is the house he bought because the ghost of Pearline was everywhere in our family home:

Pearline
whose voice still greeted him when he returned home at midnight from the Working Men's Club
Oh! Yu remember yu have a yard?

Pearline
whose cooking aromas still filled the kitchen, fried garlic and onions hissing in a pan, curried goat in a pot on the stove, and his favourite – rum-soaked fruit cake baking in the oven
A likkle somet'ing for later, sweetie-pie

Pearline
whose antique cook's knife, with its smooth ivory handle, gathered dust in a draw because when he used it he could feel her strong hands sawing deep into hundreds of succulent hams, the Sunday roast, gammon

Pearline
who told me I'd inherited The Gift, passed down through generations of her mother's family: to see what others could not
They'll find yu in time, Stanley

Pearline
who suspected what I already knew but did not want to admit, even to myself: that sometimes when I was on my own, I sensed I wasn't

Pearline
whose votive candles for the dead ancestors she talked to left smoky streaks on the rosebud wallpaper over their bedroom mantelpiece

Pearline
whose favourite calypso song played itself in the middle of the night, waking Clasford in a cold sweat
> *Zombie jamboree, dat took place in a London cem-e-tery,*
> *Dey were singing 'Back to back, belly to belly,*
> *Ah don't care a damn, ah done dead already.'*

When he hung up his flannel next to her threadbare green one, stiff and brittle as old cardboard, he heard her snap back,
When it get a hole, then I'll get a new one.

When he opened the bathroom cabinet searching for aspirin, it was crammed full of her medicine bottles and lotions, ointments and tubes, bandages and plasters

When he rummaged in the wardrobe, placing the armpits of her clothes to his nose, he smelled the noxious legacy of perfume infused with chemicals that had escaped through her pores

Pearline
whose teeth still lay in a solitary clouded glass, like a deep sea shellfish, on the little table her side of the bed

Pearline
whose wig sat on its stand on the dressing table, bought when her hair fell out; and when he buried his face in it, he could still smell Jax's scalp oil

Pearline
whose slippers were under the bed; and when he tried them on, he felt the lumpy misshapings of her feet, where she painfully walked

on the sides of them, where the bunion on her left one made it stick out at the front

When he unrolled her nylon stockings, he saw the saggy stretches from knees and ankles that had swollen to twice their normal size; and when he walked along the hallway, he saw her emergency overnight case parked over by the coat stand, because it hadn't made it to the hospital in time.

My father's new bed remains in its plastic sheath. The new bath stands upended in the otherwise empty bathroom. Clothes spill out of scuffed suitcases. Towels and sheets are squashed into plastic bags. There's a tower block of old boxes: official documents from the years of marriage, houses rented, bought; letters dating back to the 1940s; the passport dated 1956 that he was always going to get renewed for that migration back home that was always 'next year' away; the birth certificates, medical cards and dental cards; and, somewhere, a death certificate.

The weight of it all bearing down on us both.

A pot of congealed stew sits on the stove; beyond being unhygienic and an attractive proposition for flies, it's now just a cold, hard, flavourless lump. The last meal he ever cooked for himself. The cooker's four-eyed face is covered with grease. The garden is a nature reserve for foxes and rats, which are the subject of complaints by the neighbours to the council, which issues threats, which he ignores.

'Hi, it's only me. It's Stanley,' I call out with enforced cheerfulness, letting him know he can drop the hammer that he's just picked up, that he's slept with for decades in case the robbers he's been expecting finally do break in. I step on to the local free newspapers, which I push to one side with my feet, aware that whatever state my father is in, his hearing is unimpaired and a row will ensue if he hears me moving things about. Nothing is to be touched, not even the stew, which is still good enough to be eaten one day, *Mi na wasteful like you perishin' youngsters with yer cash an' carry, easy come easy trowaway ways.*

He sits in a brown tweed armchair, where he also sleeps. He hasn't gone upstairs for years, and, although I bought a single bed for the sitting room, he doesn't use it. This is where he sits all day, watching the television but not taking anything in any more. The world in colourful miniature, reduced to a murmuring visual backdrop in a corner of the room: the cookery programmes and soaps, the quiz shows and chat shows, films from Hollywood, Ealing Studios, Bollywood, the make-over, managing-your-money, managing-your-mind, managing-your-relationships, managing-your-every-damned-ting-shows. Once they were a point of conversation. Now it's just company that he ignores. He gets up only to let in Kathy from Meals-on-Wheels, who brings him a hot lunch at midday with a cold supper for later, which he barely touches; Raj from the off licence, who personally delivers his supplies of whisky, beer, cigarettes and chocolate; and the home help, Winnifred, whom I pay to clean up a little, but, unable to do much of this, and old enough and kind enough to humour the old man whose suspicious eyes follow her every move, she at least keeps an eye on him every Wednesday.

I walk with caution as I enter the sitting room, seeing first the commode that is only a few feet from him, and even then sometimes too far away. The gas fire is on. Winter. Summer. Spring. The windows are never opened. It's beyond being stuffy. It's an inferno.

He sits behind the door.

I feel the squelch of piss beneath my feet.

I sit down on the bed, which runs along the right-hand wall, placing a newspaper over it first.

'How are you?' Of course this is the most ridiculous question of all, but I can't help myself.

'Not good, not bad.' Sometimes it's 'Not too bad' or 'Could be better' or 'Not bad, not good' or, on really bad days, 'Don't ask!'

My immediate impulse is, as always, to embark on clearing everything up, to get one gargantuan black dustbin bag and chuck the whole bloody room in it – including him. There's that old globe of his, for a start, sitting on the mantelpiece, all smoke-stained and sun-bleached from the days when he let daylight into the room.

The countries and borders are about thirty years out of date. He made me memorize every country in the world when I was a boy and whacked me if I got one wrong. *The bloody noses, the split lips, the purple eyes, the zipped-up lips, the chill in his voice, my head down. Thank you, for your words in my useless mouth, for your early-morning rises, your sacrifices. Yes, I promise to obey you unto kingdom come and I will never, ever let you down after all you've done, for thou art righteous and I am, well, I am only ca-ca. your son. Amen.*

He resists every time I pick something up to be thrown away. Empty envelopes, cans, bottles, remnants of orange juice, cartons of meals, old newspapers. 'Stop rushin' me,' he'll say, because in the silent-movie space of this room, the energy of someone from the outside world of technicolour is overwhelming. After half an hour or so, I will attempt to empty the commode, then slowly drop detritus into a bag, shaking cans and bottles with great exaggeration first, right in front of him, to prove that there's not a wasteful drop left, prompting him to say, 'Doan be so *blasted* facetious.'

He'll insist the bag should be used again, once the rubbish has been emptied into the bin outside.

He hasn't washed in years; he won't let me or anyone else touch him. His nails grow and grow and grow, until they break off into jagged edges. His hair and beard, no longer dyed black, grow and grow and grow, into tangled scouring brushes. His trousers are stained with urine, his mouth dehydrated, with the dead skin on his loose lips forming little molluscs. He doesn't smell as much as the room, though, because, like the stew outside, the germs die after a while. They say that after the first few years the dirt doesn't get any worse.

Should I wash him? Maybe I should force him. It is obscene, washing my father.

How can I, his son, wash his balls?

Reaching out to my father, but with each lunge his body drifts off out of my grip, floating upwards; his big bones have lost their fleshy padding.

I am calling him down, to come back to me, *please* come back to me, but my words are muffled by water and the current is drifting him away and the creatures of the deep are swimming around us, oblivious as they dart in and out of the sodden timbers

the floating net curtains, tentacles trailing like colourless ribbons, are Sea Wasps; shoals of Clupeid Fry are electrified flying nails recruited from all the fallen doors and creaking floorboards of this house

the weird colony of yellowy sac-like Sea Squirts resembles the tapioca pudding delivered by Meals-on-Wheels, which he hates and always leaves

on the floor are piles of fresh diarrhoea, the Sea Cucumber, which I sometimes have to scoop up for him; it eats sand, in the hope of finding edibles inside

the luminous pink wisps of the Sea Slug, the violet-tipped polyps of the amorphous beings of the living coral

then we enter the dark zone, the cold zone, the abysmal abyssal plane, I try to catch him, but he is lost to me now, as he disappears over the top of the largest mountain range in the world, beneath the continental shelf in the forbidding basin, his wasted legs paddling as his brown corduroy slacks fall down, his feet limp and crusty at the heels

I am no anchor; he is supposed to be mine, he is going, going . . .

and I am left only with the creatures of the deep that I watch on videos late at night when I can't sleep, because I can lose myself in their magical world for hours

here mouth ulcers hover in the water like Christmas baubles with brilliant lights radiating from inside unused condoms twirl around in a strange ballet with ET eyes, with a ballerina's swirling tutu skirt of red skin for a behind, bought when he imported a woman from home, a 'pen pal' who never wrote once she left this house

here there are beings that need no hard protective skin because there are no solid surfaces; his brain cells are afloat in alcohol, creatures whose skeletons show like X-rays beneath a layer of fragile transparency

they are looking for prey; I am praying for him

and then he drifts back down, through the ceiling, head first like a deep sea diver, arms at his side, feet flapping, and finds his way back into his armchair, bubbles coming out of his nose, and he picks up a can of beer and pours its remains into the dirty mug that reads:

40 YEARS — PEARLINE & CLASFORD — RUBY

He lights a cigarette as if he's been nowhere, nowhere at all, and suddenly, noticing the look of exasperation on my face, he snaps, 'Is all I've got left.'

'But it's so bad for you. It's killing you.'

'Doan be ridiculous. Nuttin' no wrong with it. Doan believe the papers. Go get my supplies, son.'

I get him to sign his pension book. His signature is all indecipherable swirls curling into each other, like an elaborate doodle – to deter counterfeit, although now it takes longer to create this intricate artwork.

Hidden in his signature is my father, somewhere.

Heaven, Really

Bone white, white lead, blond, *blanc d'argent, blanc de fard, blanc fixe*, antimony white, titanium white, strontium white, Paris white, zinc oxide, zinc sulphide.

Before I moved into this place and redecorated I never knew there were so many official shades of white. When I get back home, stepping into my flat is like stepping on to a moving cloud, into heaven, really. If I don't watch it, I'll fall down, because the floor is an optical illusion and hardly there at all. My place is just white with sloping attic ceilings and nothing on the walls or surfaces. No ornaments or adornments to show my wealth or taste, or lack of it. No magazines to show I'm hip to popular culture or my esoteric erudition. No books to show off my catholic literary interests. No letters, photos, sentimental mementoes, such as my first comic book or old school tie. No plants to show I'm a nurturing kinda guy, and certainly no moulting quadrupeds, thank you very much. (Though I sometimes think a limply aristocratic Dalmatian would fit in nicely – on a cream rug, just there underneath the window – so long as it doesn't move.)

Pure emptiness. Just the way I like it. Cheap too. Sophistication on a budget. The bare minimum of soft furnishings in contrasting shades, well, in the words of my design manual, 'subtle complementary tones of white'; while my two lounge windows, at this level, provide mutable art works that cost nothing. My favourite painting comes at least once a year: it's called January Snow Blizzard.

There is nothing more beautiful than a marble mantelpiece and fire surround, offset by ivory painted walls, with the sun pouring in and splashing everything with a warm orange glow. Nothing more beautiful than squares of snow-white floorboards, pearl-white skirting and an eggshell sofa throw, with flake-white cushions on it. Nothing more exquisite than an occasional wooden table painted off-white and, upon this, my occasional deviant indulgence: a single Van Gogh sunflower in a slim glass vase. A solitary sunflower that draws you in while standing out, a potent symbol of life and, as the week progresses, decay. In other homes a great bunch of magnolias mixed with carnations mixed with roses mixed with tulips mixed with branches and leaves and whatnots is stuffed into an ostentatious vase and completely loses any possible charm amid all the chaos of clashing colours and a room full of things, things and things. I am 'cos I have bloody things!

Here, a single flower is what I call – resonant.

In my narrow kitchen everything is hidden in white cupboards, except a Chinese-white porcelain bowl of oranges, pears, apples and grapes. And when they go mouldy, brown or bruise, what is it? Pure modern art, man. The whole flat is a gallery and I am but a walking sculpture inside it. A solitary sculpture, yet to find its perfect match. And she'd have to look good lounging on my sofa. No one ever does – they just mess it up. Sometimes, months later, I'll find evidence underneath the sofa or down in between the seat cushions, such as a thread of hair, split at the end – strawberry blonde at the bottom and chestnut at the top, or a thick straightened brown one going frizzy at the root, or just a tiny black curl in my palm, like a perfect circle drawn with ink. When they leave, I have to open the windows, straighten out the room and light candles.

The Paragon: 'A model of supreme excellence, it was completed in 1807. The year that Blackheath achieved the status of a fashionable and elegant place to live. Replete with every convenience for use, comfort and elegance. A place to attract well-to-do professional and middle-class families who want to enjoy the air of the heath.' So I've arrived, living in the upper echelons of this crescent of houses with its own secluded road.

I start to clean, wiping all the surfaces with a wet cloth, washing the windows on the inside; then I lean dangerously out on the ledge and clean the outside too. I polish the TV and sound system, and run a duster over the CD rack, all stacked away in a cupboard. I hoover the floor, before getting down on my hands and knees to give it a good sloshing with some hot soapy water and bleach. Next, the kitchen, the bathroom and my bedroom at the back with its semicircular window, just large enough for a double bed and a built-in wardrobe (all white).

When I'm done, my flat might not look much different but it certainly feels it. I draw a bath and soak in lavender oil, get up, drain it out and check to see if I've left a rim of scum behind. I like to see evidence that my dirt has gone. If not, I scratch off all the dead skin with a loofah, shower and then shampoo my hair until it squeaks. Finally, I put on my white cotton pyjamas, place all the clothes I've worn to my father's house in the washing machine, hose down the soles of my pissy shoes and begin to cook. Well, I heat up something in the microwave, something ready-made from the supermarket, a cheesy tuna pasta today, and I make a lemon, garlic, mustard, honey, herb and oil dressing for a green leaf salad.

I sit down in front of the TV, pick out my favourite video and slide it into the video recorder. *The Great Barrier Reef* – 'a sea-girt wilderness of coral reefs, cays, islands and sheltered seas, forming a one hundred thousand square mile fringe of the eastern Australian mainland'.

Flying to Tower Hamlets

Next Saturday I call to say I'm on my way. He doesn't pick up.

I don't notice the drive to his house or the red lights. My siren is blaring. I try to open the door, but the key won't fit. It's the wrong key. My hands won't fit. They're the wrong hands. Then the key does fit, but it won't turn. It's the wrong lock. It's the wrong door. It's the wrong house. Then the key turns, but the door won't budge. So I push against it with my shoulder and it suddenly gives way and I'm thrown inside as if I've just crossed the finishing line in a tremendous last-ditch burst of power and agility and my legs are flying behind me trying to catch up. I stumble towards his room, then stop myself.

I take a deep breath and open the door.

He's on the floor. He's paralytic on the floor, arms and legs splayed out like a crab's. For Christ's sake it's only bloody eleven in morning. Couldn't he have waited until the afternoon before passing out? Ever heard of a solid breakfast, Dad? Remember the days when you ate porridge from a saucepan every morning without fail? Not something liquid and fermented?

I bend over him and shake his shoulder. He stirs and mumbles something. Nothing new there. I really struggle to lift him because he's a dead weight and I've never lifted a dead weight off the floor before, so my body is twisting one way and his another as I drag him on to his chair. He's wet himself, and he's drooling, and his eyes are swimming, and there's a bump on his head.

He's not drunk. Jesus Christ, he's not drunk!

I dial 999.

Suspected dehydration, they tell me at the hospital. Dehydration, pure and simple. Hydrate him, then, I say, relieved. I don't think he's drunk a glass of water for years.

I go home and resume work on my Toshiba laptop, researching Thai government bonds that do not have sufficient history to make investment expectations certain.

The hospital calls me at midnight.

The doctor's voice is middle aged, middle class, tired, measured, concerned, practised, ever so slightly hesitant, anonymous and unforgettable.

'Can I speak to Mr Stanley Williams, please?'

'Speaking.'

'I am sorry to call you so late . . .'

The Coroner's Office

Brain	1,230g
R. Lung	375g
L. Lung	750g
Heart	270g .
Liver	1,120g
Spleen	135g
R. Kidney	135g
L. Kidney	135g

The body was that of a thin elderly man of Afro-Caribbean race, 166cm in height, at the time of my examination unclothed.

The pleural spaces were clear. There were dense bilateral inter-pleural and pleuropericardial adhesions with hyaline plaques on the diaphragm. The air passages contained abundant pus and were inflamed. The lungs were congested and oedematous and showed pneumonic consolidation affecting in particular the lower lobe of the left lung with severe chronic inflammatory thickening of the bronchial tree. There was a slight thickening of the dilation of pulmonary arteries. No evidence of thromboembolism.

Remarks:	Death due to natural causes
Cause of Death:	1a Bronchopneumonia
	1b Chronic obstructive airways disease
Time of Death:	11.55 p.m. 29.8.1987
Time of Examination:	10.35 a.m. 1.9.1987

Dr Amanda Foster, MD, MRCPath, Dip FMSA (Belg.), DMJ
Department of Forensic Medicine

The Burial Ground

Stanley is burying his father, in a field of dumb bedfellows whose sole purpose is to provide balanced nutrition for the more vulnerable members of the animal kingdom: the invertebrates, who eat with the slow, sarcastic knowledge that dinner really isn't going *anywhere*. These are the subterranean militia of revenge, whose communal memory stores the cruel holocaust of their various insect species by predictable versions of swat: shoe, garden implement, rolled-up newspaper, cricket bat.

Mr Clasford Williams is the newest, fully paid-up resident of Tower Hamlets' community of gourmet cadavers, whose social relationship to each other is defined only by proximity and the fact that their hearts, in one breathtaking moment, had stopped.

Here Clasford will crave his daily cocktail of whisky and beer, as rainwater soaks through his rotting oak coffin with its oyster-coloured lining, through the linen safari suit he'd brought with him in 1965, *When mi fus come a this blasted country,* and finally seeps down to accentuate his thirst and accelerate the decay of brown skin that had been, for thirty-two years, his formal application to British society, determining his acceptance or rejection, something he was always going on about. *We doan belong ina this country . . . we doan belong, Stanley.* The bitterness at his transformation from fully qualified chemist in his home country to ill-paid postman in his adopted one never quite overcome. Clasford had overseen the trajectory of Stanley from grammar school boy, to university graduate, to City analyst receiving a weekly pay cheque that Clasford himself could never earn in a whole month of rising at 4 a.m. to sort out the post at the depot. But if it was a slap on the back Stanley craved: 'Ongle a man like me can produce pickney like oonoo. So don't swell y'head and tink say y'boots bigger than mine.'

'Hardly likely,' Stanley would mutter.

To which Clasford would reply, drawing his arm back as if to hit him, 'Awa you say?'

'Nuttin'.' Stanley shuffled out of the room, letting his father have the last word, as always, as he walked down the corridor.

'Leave the bwai alone, Clasford,' his mother interjected. 'Mi know say yuh proud like lion fer im. We *both* are, Stanley,' she shouted out as Stanley slammed his bedroom door.

'I shoulda let him roam street. Woulda end up in the chink by now,' added Clasford, topping Pearline in volume.

Now, when Clasford turned over in his sleep towards the heavenly body of Pearline, who had preceded him underground, when he reached out to caress her ample, blue-nylon softness, she would not respond warmly to him with a cajoling 'You tink yu can manage it, Ole Bwai?' or resist with sleepy irritation: 'Mi not in the *mood*, Clasford!'

Pearline, who was lying peacefully beside him, had turned into an unappetizing arrangement of celibate bones. Nor would he sweat at night, as he had done all his married life, drenching the sheets, so that Pearline would complain that he'd give her rheumatism 'one-a these days'.

Storm clouds had been rallying forces all morning on this windswept east London plateau. Its sprawling perimeter was over-hung by trees with wrinkled brown, rust and golden leaves that floated to the ground. In the distance were tower blocks, which rendered an otherwise pastoral scene inescapably urban. The city fathers converged, broke off into splinter groups and flaunted their double-breasted chests, puffed up with the arrogance of knowing that a few dobs of well-aimed spittle were enough to warn the mourners below of their omnipotence.

Stanley wished the sky would split open into a terrible storm, wished for hailstones and lightning, for weather so dramatic that the feelings raging inside him would be matched, indeed dwarfed, indeed erased, by the roaring elements. He wore a specially bought new black suit purchased the day before, and his long legs were astride the heap of earth beside the hole into which the coffin had been lowered; inside was the man he had last seen in the mortuary's viewing room, who had made him feel, for the first time in his life, infernally mortal.

He had entered the small, pine-panelled room with the atmospheric mood lighting of a chapel. Its background music was the hum of an air conditioner, and there was a flashing red light on the wall, specially designed for dead bodies on display. In the far corner was a vase containing a spray of violet lilacs and white lilies on an elegant metal plinth.

As he crossed the threshold, his body shrank like a cartoon figure's, losing two thirds of its height and bulk, disappearing into too-big clothes and shuffling in grown-up shoes. Unthinkingly, the unbroken voice of his childhood squeaked, 'Hello, Daddy', accompanied by a wild deluge of tears.

Stanley was immediately immersed in the most intimate communion with the man before whom he would never, ever cry.

Clasford Williams was tucked up into a purple drape with gold crosses embroidered on its sides. His head rested on a white pillow. His face, a dark matt brown, was so old yet so unlined, skin moulded smoothly over cheekbones that lack of food had made overly prominent, and his tensile jawline was as stubborn in death as it had been in life. His wild grey bush of hair had been cut close to his head, his wild grey beard had been trimmed into a neat goatee. His lips, which in his last years drooped listlessly away from his few remaining bottom teeth, had been tightly tucked in by the undertaker, making them thinner. His face still exuded a restrained fierceness, for after only a few days of death his body still contained something of the spirit that had been within him. Surely this is what Stanley could sense – or did the life force that made eyes shine with light from the miracle of creation, that gave skin its sheen, really just disappear so quickly, without even a lingering trace, after over seventy years? Just like that?

Clasford did not turn his head as he entered. Stanley half expected him to. He expected his usual brusque manner, for his voice to say with the familiar tone that carried both threat and approval with measured weight, 'Mi know oonoo bin behavin' yerself.' But he ignored him. Not a lopsided smile. Not a rant. Not a reprimand or provocation. Stanley moved closer. Here was death at close range. He touched his father's brow fleetingly; it was deep-frozen. Two slits of eyes showed spookily beneath his closed lids. They hadn't shut them properly.

Stanley's urge was to pick him up in his big arms and cradle him. Would he be stiff and light? He would be cold. Would he melt as he held him, turn back to water and pour himself over his son?

He looked so frail. So dignified. So.

He sat down on the seat at the side. A box of tissues had been provided on a little table, and he was overwhelmed with a compassion that he never knew was in him. 'I'm so sorry,' he cried aloud. 'I'm so sorry, Daddy.'

He sat there and let it all flow out of him, wanting to stay close to his father's presence, which had always been there. Like air. Like memory. Like skin. Like earth. Like birth. Like the ghostly presences he had felt ever since he could remember – curtains blowing, the tingling in his ears, the cold breath down his spine, the breeze on his lips, a whisper. Realizing that now he would feel his father even more acutely.

Realizing he was only human after all.

Single at Mingles, 1988

There were dancers, in various stages of electrocution, who jerked knees and elbows on the lightning floor as the disco ball above their heads conferred a swirling galaxy, the strobe turning dandruff into luminescent stars and cheap white suits fluorescent with radiation.

Each new detonation from the stacked boom boxes in the four corners of the disco was the Big Bang of the universe, as James Brown's 'Sex Machine' sent the Friday-nighters into renewed paroxysms. Neon-pink talons and conveyor-belt diamonds waved in the smoky air. Gold-sovereign'd fists punched out at the inter-stellar chaos that poured through them, over them and under them.

Stanley: I'd been hijacked after work and frog-marched by the guys to this bunker called Mingles, where I squinted in the searchlight of a crazed strobe, my laced-up brogues stamped on by feet hopping to detonating beats that ricocheted around the fragile, membranous chamber encasing the one solid asset I was purported to own: my brain.

Behind the bar Jessie O'Donnell groaned inwardly as more tipsy revellers in fake Miami tans tumbled down the stairs in black satin pants and white stilettos, shutting out the flashing carousels, screeching dodgems and general helter-skelter of Piccadilly's midnight circus outside.

This is what I've come to, she nagged away at herself, pulling, squirting, plunging and pouring various types of alcohol into various shapes of glass. This is the fag end of a career treading the boards. An entertainer, an *artiste*, even, some would say, a diva.

What was she now? A barmaid. At *her* age.

Stanley: I slunked against the wall, my damp fingers slid into the grooves of a pint-sized mug, sipped beer at tepid intervals, felt the gradual lightness in my head and that heavy sinking feeling in my belly, as people poured in from the street – like vomit – and the music vibrated on my sternum, making me feel sick and HATE-HAVING-TO-SHOUT-TO-SPEAK.

Jessie longed to see nothing but long, empty roads in front of her. To take four wheels, a credit card and the hitherto elusive *compañero*.

But there were more sparkling white wines to serve, more Babychams, Bacardis, beery breaths and Bloody Marys. More – 'ere, got any chips? *No!* Tapas? *No!* Twiglets? *No!* You're a big girl, aren't you? *Bugger off or I'll call Security!*

Stanley: My body is a stubborn bastard, it won't do those strange, rhythmical manoeuvres fuelled by the human need for exhibitionism and abandonment, and even if it did the whole dance floor would crease up and covertly imitate, just like my first and last disco for the Tower Hamlets Under Sixteens (prompting premature retirement from this particular form of brain–body coordination).

Gloria Gaynor's 'I Will Survive' hit the decks. The ultimate crowd pleaser, it was still the personal anthem for those who'd been dumped and wanted revenge, and those who planned on doing the dumping.

Stanley: So there I was – Stanley Orville Cleve Williams – who was supposed to be doing his *thang*, only he didn't know what his *thang* was.

So I dodged my way to the bar to replenish myself.

Jessie was this close to walking out when, looking to her right, she found herself glaring at a young man who was smiling back at her. Cheeky thing. How dare he.

Stanley: That's when the barmaid caught my eye.

Still, he *was* waiting patiently for her to serve him at the end of the bar. Manners. Lot to be said for it. She kept her eyes on him, surprised that he didn't look away intimidated. Instead he looked amused. She found herself resisting a sudden urge to smile back.

Young, copper-toned, crew-cut, cleanly shaven – she thought he looked too freshly scrubbed for the setting of Mingles. He wore a pale blue office shirt and a dark blue tie with gold flashes and no ring to show that he'd been tamed and made (theoretically) monogamous.

What a lovely young puppy dog.

'What's your poison?' Jessie called out, ignoring the fisted fivers thrust in her face by agitated customers.

'You!' he shouted back, grinning.

The club went into filmic, soft-focus, slow-motion. The faint glockenspiel of glasses. The harmonics of subdued voices. She beckoned him over with a seductive index finger, drawing him into her magnetic field:

Be – Lauren Bacall.
        Be – Mae West.
                Be – Eartha Kitt.
                        Miaaooowww . . .

And she whorishly deliquesced.

Café Italia, Soho

'I'm forty-five, but look thirty. Not vanity but fact, Stanley, dear. Wish I was twenty, if I knew then what I know now, etc. Have the emotional age of a three-year-old, or so every man I've ever married felt obliged to inform me. I've got the life experience of an octogenarian and a veiled woman going by the name of Salomé at the funfair at Roundhay Park, who, I may say, looked suspiciously like Mary O'Reilly what used to run chippie in Leeds High Street, told me I'd see in my ninety-ninth year, God forbid. Now, Stanley, when you boldly stared me out at Mingles. Sixteen. I was definitely sixteen again. Does that answer your question?'

Stanley and Jessie were seated on high stools beside each other in Soho's Café Italia, which was crammed with late-night revellers with bloodshot eyes and boisterous chatter. Sinatra, Stallone, Capone – a gallery of expensive suits lined the stairs, their all-Italian-American smiles shining like beacons for those en route to the toilet. The décor hadn't changed much since the 1950s: green and yellow linoleum tiles and long-panelled mirrors, which they were staring into while sipping copious amounts of the best cappuccino in town.

Jessie wore a low-cut blue chiffon blouse with a sheepskin jacket draped glamorously over her shoulders. On closer observation, its furry collar could be seen to be suffering from alopecia. Hazel-coloured eyes were her most noticeable feature, kohl eyeliner smudged on with casual affectation. They were smoky, vaguely bemused, secretive, and they appeared to look in on themselves rather than pay attention to the world outside, although, as with Marlene Dietrich, the world outside was drawn to look in on them. If her eyes were not those of an innocent, her complexion was the unlined, hazelnut-brown of a woman half her age. Plumptious lips, remnants of maroon lipstick staining the corners, were petulant. Long plait extensions were tied up with a black velvet scrunchie on top of her head and spilled chaotically over Rubenesque shoulders.

While Jessie was fascinated with her own reflection, so too was Stanley, he couldn't take his eyes off her. He thought her extraordinarily dramatic-looking, sexily fleshy, giving as good as she got to the customers at Mingles, which he had found hilarious. She appeared to him now through the mirror as a gorgeous mirage.

His was an archetypal Caribbean face, which others found attractive but at which he could not look without being appalled at how dull it was. A face waiting for someone to move in and mess it up a bit, he thought, not realizing it was already loaded with the cargo of many seafarers. Bright slanting eyes, inherited from some hapless boy who had sailed from the island of Macao to decades of indentured labour on a sugar plantation in the faraway West Indies. A broad, shining forehead was the legacy of an ancestor who had lain in the hold of a galleon that sailed due west, cutting a swath between waves that rose like Turner's white flames. And the thin mouth of an aristocratic Scottish planter, vulnerable top lip rising like the tip of a wave over his slipstreamed bottom lip, indicating just a hint of self-pity.

Conversation was easy.

'How could I ever forget sixteen. School trip to Blackpool and that Curtis from the boys' home. Had my Terry nine months later; he's in Australia now. When he was younger, I used to slip out to do my turn in a cabaret or pub, sneak back in and there he was, good as gold, still sleeping. Couldn't do that these days, could you? Get done by Welfare. Got a card from him – Christmas last.'

My darling boy,
you were smitten, once.

Lovely liquid eyes helpless
fixed on mine, until
you fell asleep, smiling,
tiny, podgy feet
wriggling warmly
in my hot palms.

Couldn't live without me, once.
Penny-for-a-song funds
paying for your all-in-ones,
milk-laden jugs at your lips,
devoted heart ready
to kill anyone who'd harm yer.

Were lost to each other,
me and thee.

Were made for each other,
me and thee,

out of nothing
but an escaped seed
finding its way home.

Jessie's eyes wandered over to Stanley's through the mirror, where they watered. He noticed a shift, tried to hold them long enough to get the measure of it, but she slipped out of reach, looked down at her coffee and took a sip. She wiped a deposit of froth from her lips, manoeuvring her tongue so slowly that Stanley could barely restrain himself from leaning over to meet his tongue with hers. When she finally looked back up, her eyes were clear and confident again.

He swung over to his own reflection and did a double-take: his face was preternaturally radiant. He was beaming. And it wasn't forced at all.

She resumed the conversation and blew a strong gust of coffee-breath at him. He inhaled it deeply.

A Brewster Montgomery had been her mentor, she told him. A mature man whose offer of marriage to this single mother was heaven-sent, a man who knew how to temper her teenage explosions and treat her child as his own. A black American trumpeter who had arrived in Britain with the US Army during the Second World War, Brewster ran the Off Beat Jazz Club in a basement in Soho Square. He encouraged her nascent singing ambitions, allowing her to open acts but never treating her as an equal. She didn't complain. She loved Terry.

Stanley soaked up Jessie's husky Yorkshire vowels – a voice so different to his own flatter, neutral, London tones.

It was a sticky Sunday night at the Off Beat when Brewster had the heart attack he always looked like he was having when he blew his horn, she told Stanley, dramatizing with facial gestures, cheeks unbelievably inflated, eyes almost popping out on two springs like an animation, temple about to give birth to worms. She froze, milking Terry at the back of the club, while the tragedy played itself out through a broth of cigarette smoke, clashing perfumes, sweat, and the steam of spirits, ales and wines. She found herself wondering if her husband actually owned the club or merely rented it.

'I returned home pot-less, worked my singing apprenticeship in grotty late-night pubs before graduating to the Northern club circuit.'

She tapped her feet against his shins. Her legs were sheathed in red slacks. She kept crossing and uncrossing them while he peeked at the voluptuous spread of her thighs. The musky scent of patchouli oil floated his way. When it didn't, he sniffed it out. He studied her plump, smooth hands, wanting to stroke them, imagining they would be a little spongy. He saw the way her fingers tapered slimly off into pastel-pink nail polish – discreetly chipped. She wore an antique gold ring with a ruby, which he imagined had been a gift, perhaps from this Brewster person. When she touched him to emphasize a point – a knee, a shoulder, a hand – she lingered, perhaps longer than was necessary, he wasn't sure; she seemed to flash danger at him, as if daring him to respond. With each touch, he felt a palpitating charge, like a mild burn on his skin.

Stanley moved his stool closer to hers under the guise of shuffling into a more comfortable position. Their knees were now squashed up together.

She started to sing through the mirror, surprising him so much that he just about suppressed a burst of laughter. Hers was the coarse, booming voice of a knackered troubadour. She flung open her arms with all the melodramatic pathos of a Judy Garland, oblivious to the stares and nudges from the other people in the coffee bar. *'Moon river . . . My funny valentine . . . Some enchanted evening . . .'*

Without moving his head, Stanley nervously scanned the crowd. When he noticed their response shift from snickering shock to open admiration and rapidly thereon to audience participation, he relaxed into a grin that claimed pride and partnership in the ruckus Jessie was creating.

'For years I hoped that one day I'd be rooted out by a record producer, but big wigs in the industry never deigned to come up to the Bletchington Working Men's Club or the Middleton-in-Teesdale Social Society Annual Christmas Cabaret.'

Whether she could sing well was by the by: she was a black woman with the novelty of a Northern accent infused with what she imagined was a Texan drawl, making every interminable note twang with vibrato like a reverberating mouth harp. She was fond of vibratos. Truth is, she *looked* like everyone's idea of a soul diva – a Gladys Knight, Roberta Flack, Gloria Gaynor – with large breasts that she liked to promote so that they rippled like the surface of a pond. But she turned mellow torch songs into raucous rock numbers and, thinking that she was displaying virtuosity, damaged her voice by pushing it once too often out of its natural range, imagining herself another Jessye Norman or Lulu as her mouth opened wide enough for the Hebden Bridge Brass Band to march through.

She bounced down off the stool, threw on her coat and, before Stanley could decide whether to object, steered him by the shoulders out of Café Italia and into the cold night. She linked his arm with hers and huddled into him, precipitating an unexpected torrent of sweat that ran down his back to gather in a pool just above his belt.

'Let's walk to mine. It's not often I get to walk through London in the early hours. You can only do it with a male accomplice, really.'

She led him through the cramped streets of Soho, past the Chinese groceries and eateries and the trashy strip-joints and peep-shows; they cut through the glare of Leicester Square, still buzzing with tourists and clubbers and indiscreet street walkers. Entering the quieter refinement of Long Acre, they strolled into Covent Garden, across the cobblestones of the deserted Italianate piazza by St Paul's Church, down by the side of the market, into Southampton Street, then on to the Strand, heading east.

Whenever Stanley tried to lead, Jessie speeded up so that he was always half a step behind. He didn't mind. He wasn't noticing anything much except the sensation of the body that was rubbing up against his side.

'That Harley Street specialist told me never to sing again. So I turned my hand to comedy. Do you think it was easy getting up on stage and telling gags in 1970? I was shot down on account of my colour or gender or the size of my protuberances or usually all three by those bastards. So it became no-holds-barred expletives and jokes of the lewdest nature.'

. . . *All heart and humour, that's me,*
bombastic, wise-cracking, ballsy bitch,

up there on stage giving it large,
like my sole mission on this planet

is to make them crack up
so's they forget their sorry little lives.

But what about mine, eh?
What about my rumbling stomach,

my hole in the flamin' breakin' bleedin'
no-one-gives-a-damn-do-they-heart?

Where's my handyman-cum-plumber,
my caretaker, welder, electrician,

what won't short-circuit me for a change?
You see, no sod'll go the distance,

not when he's been sold a go-getter,
then creeps out of bed one night

to find me slid down the bathroom wall,
a snivelling heap of snot on the floor.

'The eighties blew in and with it that craze called alternative comedy. All of a sudden my mullet-headed, baccy-chewing great god of an agent Wyn McGregor acquired one of those new-fangled things called an answer-phone and that was that. Miss wearing my best bib and tucker, Stanley. Still do, to this day.'

'Of course you miss the adulation too.'

Jessie stiffened and snapped, 'Freud now, is it?'

When Stanley looked hurt instead of rising to the bait, she found her anger subsiding. Maybe she wouldn't have to fight this one. She was so tired of fighting.

. . . Had to be a warrior in those days,
attack or end up in the asylum,

like other early-born blacks up North.
Before immigration *en masse*

we were few in number
and often outnumbered – by thugs.

Got no back-up then, no fancy
Race Relations Department at Council.

More than once I stood on the precipice.
Couldn't wash – me or the dishes,

dragged my feet to the shops only when
the last tin of spaghetti in tomato sauce ran out,

but I wasn't going to end up another nutter
drooling in the loony bin,

pills for breakfast, lunch and tea.
So I got a doctor's certificate, a visa

allowing me to leave a country
called Clinica Depressia

for a paradise island called Valium –
were a lovely holiday, went away for years.

Won't be telling Stanley any of this.
Whatever you tell them at the start

will be used as evidence against you
at the end, your honour . . .

'That's what you crave when you're an entertainer,' she said. 'You miss the anticipation, the adrenalin. Everybody adores you and then one day you turn around and no one's behind you.'

'I'm sure plenty of men have adored you.' Stanley realized he had some repair work to do. He'd never met a temperamental artiste before, although he'd heard they all were. Everyone he knew worked in an office and wore a suit to work.

'Yes, my cousin, for a start.'

'What?'

'I married my cousin.'

'Why?'

'Don't be daft, I didn't know he was, did I? Look, I was a foundling. Left outside Leeds General Infirmary – raised in St Ann's Children's Home. The home was full of the North's half-caste rejects. Anyway, along comes Kwame many lonely years after Brewster died. Half-caste, Leeds man. Loves young Terry. Young Terry loves him. We look alike too, and they say you go for people who look like yourself. So we get married and he says he wants to know what diseases are in my genes, for when we have kids. I'm scared as hell, but he badgers me and I discover that my father was a certain Kojo Mensah, who came looking for me when I was a toddler. A student at Leeds, apparently. Never told Welfare who my mother was, so that I'll never know. The punch line is, Stanley, that Kwame's surname was Mensah. Our fathers were brothers. Both men got their degrees, went home to Ghana, never to be heard of again.

'We tried to continue, but you can't, can you? No way forward, no way back.'

'That's terrible,' said Stanley, stopping in his tracks, attempting to gather her into his arms.

'That's life, and I don't need any pity, love,' she replied, pulling back, before adding with more gentleness, 'I don't dwell on the past, me.'

Locked him up where he's safe,
still a young man in his late twenties,
not handsome but dapper
with his painstakingly pruned moustache.

He'll never age, my Kwame,
no grey roots ruining his curly perm.
He always used too much grease:
Here let me wring yer head out,
I want to fry some chips!

Bought this tasselled suede jacket
from Carnaby Street in *London.*
He'd nowhere special to go in it.
We'd curl up on the settee for *Coronation Street*
and play with his tassels.

Kwame remembered
birthdays, valentines, anniversaries.
He'd take my hand and Terry's hand
every time we went out,
so's you could tell we were a family.

'Right now I work for another one of my ex's, Mr Roderick Wilson, during the day, and I suffer Mingles at weekends. Rod's set himself up with another business, Mullineaux & Merryweather, Dealers of Antiques, in Ridley Road Market, Hackney. In between Hyacinth's Caribbean Grocers and Allah's Halal Butchers. It's a pettifoggin' junk shop, Stanley, and my sales pitch is making him bucket loads. *Madam, this beautifully ornate piss pot is genuine seventeenth century.* Nice bit of commission on the side for me. Calais here I come!'

At Clerkenwell they turned off Farringdon Road into Cherry Tree Court, a short, narrow road with no trees and no court. Houses with the gaunt faces of dying old men lined each side. They had been divided into flats and bedsits. Jessie waved to the house she lived in. He looked up at the tall building with its peeling paintwork. Yet, instead of inviting him in, to his disappointment she pointed out an olive-green Lada Niva 4-Wheel Drive parked outside.

'Here's Matilda, my trusty jeep.' She patted the rusty bonnet. 'Not find a more reliable motor than her. Has a knack of breaking down right next to a garage.'

It's not a jeep, Stanley wanted to say. And it's got eczema. He looked at the passenger seat, which was strewn with scrunched-up fish and chip newspaper, red ketchup sachets and a crushed can of Coca-Cola. She picked it all up and chucked it on to the back seat.

'Tell you what, fancy a spin down to the coast? How about Broadstairs-sur-la-Mer?'

She got into the driver's seat and started the engine, revving it so loudly he was sure she'd woken up the whole street.

'Well, come on. Gerrin in, if you're coming.'

He'd never thought of driving down to the coast, on impulse or otherwise. It felt so daring. He felt ridiculous. He climbed in and they drove off across London.

For the first time since they had met, Jessie was completely silent.

. . . Oh but that elongated flicker
of devotion at Mingles,
some disenchanted evening
full of perma-tanned drunks.
Just who pops up over my counter
like jack-in-the-box.

Who gets served first, tells me
to keep the change.
Who'll be my baby-rattle, my dearest boy,
my rocking-cradle-joy.

And when I turn around,
he'll be gurgling sweetly, hopefully.

They reached the Blackwall Tunnel, beyond which lay the suburbs of south-east London, and beyond that the open fields of Kent. They picked up the motorway at Dartford and drove into the countryside. Stanley sat upright, staring ahead, as if he couldn't quite believe he was doing this; but, as he was, he didn't quite know what to say or do next.

Jessie exhaled long and loud.

'A sky. A road. Going somewhere. Me, I'm a gadabout at heart. Going to drive across Europe to Australia, Stanley. The old Magic Bus route via Iran, Afghanistan and Pakistan to India, then a hop, skip, land, ferries and God knows what all the way down under. Matilda will take me. Stop off in Spain first. There's money to be made on that coast. You coming with me?'

Turning towards her, Stanley spluttered, 'Australia? Are you serious?'

'Or are you going to become one of the world's *if onlys*?'

Adopting a gently mocking tone, she added, 'If only I'd gone with that daredevil Jessie when I was younger instead of building papier mâché castles in the air. Look at me, the stock market crashed and all I've got is a caravan in Margate to retire to and double bypass heart surgery on the National Health Service waiting list.'

Slipping down into his seat, he drew his legs towards him, upturned his coat collar and disappeared beneath it.

She slid a cassette into the tape deck. Ella Fitzgerald poured out of the two crackling speakers at the back. *I've got you under my skin* . . .

'You don't have to make up your mind just yet,' she said, petting him on the knee. 'Monday morning will do. First thing, on my desk, second-in-command.'

. . . Within a few hours
my tender secret found. The boy who is shadow
to the shadow-less man.

Standing on summer's far-off sloping verge,
my sensible, black plimsoles desperate to leap
on to that last wagon of speeding, rolling stock.

Slavery, penitentiary, poverty
Hollywood's desperadoes with no choice
but to flee, or be captured, convicted,
even die, inside

childhood was a bleak litany of what-not-to-dos,
roam the streets, no
cowboys and Indians, no
scarred knees as evidence of childish adventures. I turn

my collar up, so-called chin tilted down,
and blink at this country's distant, foreign land

as we disappear
into its ancient, green appetite.

Hedges? Haystacks? Farmhouses?
Cows? Horses? Tractors?
Dark lumps become violent, predatory beasts.

How am I, city-slicker-banker-boy
supposed to know
anything

other than this weird domestic wildness,
this tame and tugging danger,
this trip into morning . . .

Broadstairs-sur-la-Mer

Mandy's Cafeteria cocked a lazy eye over the beach front at Broadstairs, a small seaside town where, Jessie informed me, old people went to die and foreign students went to learn English. As we struggled to open the car doors, hacking winds eddied in from the North Sea. The esplanade was deserted except for one brave but stupid man being dragged along by his Dobermann pinscher, his wispy white hair gone haywire as he battled against the wind. I surveyed the pebbly beach, which was rimmed with seaweed and debris from the dawn tide. It matched the stormy English Channel, which 'merged with impressionistic strokes into the sky', I declared aloud. Jessie responded by telling me to stop showing off.

Far away, where the sea ended, France began.

Mandy's sold a 'Full English Breakfast for 99p', and after over twelve hours without food we charged through the door like galloping horses with Hurricane Broadstairs at our backs. The young woman at the cash desk, her beak poking out of long, lanky hair, grimaced when we blasted cold wind into her cosy parlour. Clearly we were the first customers of the day: when we ordered the full monty, she all but stomped out into the kitchen.

'It's because we're black,' I muttered. 'See, as soon as you leave the big cities this is what you find.'

She replied with a scornful glance before muttering back, 'You can decide that or you can decide she's a sad cow and would be that way with anybody. The choice is yours, Mr Paranoid Williams.'

I was getting used to Jessie's understated ripostes.

We sat opposite each other with breakfast spread before us. I had orange squash. She ordered PG Tips, the smell of which floated pungently over to me whenever she spoke. I hadn't been in a Greasy Joe's for years because I eat fruit and muesli for breakfast – good for the brain and the bowels. I watched Jessie fold a lardy rasher of bacon on to her fork, scoop up some moist black pudding, prong a fried tomato, spear a few baked beans and crisped mushrooms, dip it all into the runny heart of an egg, then into a puddle of ketchup, stab some fried bread on to the end and stuff the lot into her mouth, leaving a tell-tale trail on her chin.

I leaned over and deftly wiped it off with my own napkin, then found myself wondering if I had just found someone to care for.

Nodding her thanks, and while still masticating, she drank some more tea and swilled the lumpy concoction around like a roaming gob-stopper before downing it; what then followed was a tremulous release of wind, of which she showed no shame. I watched as she picked up the last slice of bread, rolled it into a finger and wiped the plate clean before popping it into her mouth. Her eyes roamed over to my plate, knife and fork lying at right angles across it. I pushed it towards her, twinkling, aware that I was once again emanating preternatural radiance. She scoffed, 'What? Leftovers? Me? What do you think my name is?' Before scooping up my discarded mushrooms and sucking each finger clean with a wet smack.

I had never before met a woman so utterly determined to be herself.

I cast my mind back to my father. He would have hated Jessie.

That alone was enough to make me want to cart her off to Gretna Green or Las Vegas.

From the time I started dating, I used to imagine each girl meeting my parents. No, worse, I'd try to visualize my father's wedding speech. His best Burton's suit, relatives from back home wearing cheap imitations of last decade's fashions, confetti, super-market champagne, Mum's cholesterol-oozing wedding cake, everything. Could I see it? If not, I moved on. I guess Mum was just as hard to please. Deep down, no one would have been good enough for her son, but she never vocalized any objections.

If the truth be known, I never thought any girl could ever compare to her.

My father always wanted to find out if they were good enough for *him*. What would be his judgement, I worried, after the predictable barrage of cringe-worthy questions aimed at the unsuspecting inter-viewee? It just became easier to date passive, polite, pretty (which meant white girls or, if black, then light-skinned), safely professional (that is, no rival to his son, i.e., accountants, teachers, PAs), respectable, good provenance (What school did you go to? No, what primary school?), conservatively dressed, unimaginative, well, dullards. Rather like myself, I suppose.

Yet somewhere along this high street of relationships, with its, shall we say, takeaways, supermarkets, beauty parlours, pound-shop emporiums, cordon bleu restaurants, banks, libraries and designer boutiques, all of which I have known *intimately*, I gave up on both – marriage and love.

I became the kind of man who succumbed only to the carnal.

Now my father was gone.

I drifted back.

'The winds are quietening down to an emphysematous wheeze, are they not?' I said with mischievous flourish, just to watch Jessie pull a face and grunt, 'Do me a favour, Mr Oxford English Dictionary.'

I moved my chair over to hers, took her hand in mine. It was hot.

Her garrulousness abated while she digested breakfast. I began to answer the questions I really wanted her to ask of me.

'Listening to you talk makes me realize that I've missed out. Do you know that I didn't bunk off school once in thirteen years? I was there when the clock struck nine, my homework neatly done in exercise books uniquely unadorned with football hero stick-ons and puerile graffiti. School Report: "Stanley Williams always works to the best of his ability." Gold Star. If I had flu, my parents dosed me up and sent me in. It's the immigrant mentality. *I couldn't – so you must.* I got a First in Maths because I stayed in and worked hard when my fellow students were getting high or getting laid. Now I'm working in the City as a Quant. It's research, basically. There are only a few of us with this particular expertise, specialists *par excellence.*'

I found myself adopting the manner of an inflated banker addressing a meeting of subordinates. I never could help myself. I stretched back, extended my legs, crossed my arms behind me so that my head was supported by my hands, becoming increasingly bullish with every word.

No one had to tell me that this was where my ego, albeit precariously, nestled. It had always worked with women.

'These days, with the investment market expanding to take on a global vision, getting the paper accounts of American or European companies takes so much time. Even when you do get them, items can be defined differently due to different national laws.'

Her eyes went out of focus.

I managed to keep desperation from seeping into my voice. 'Of course, you can imagine what it's like trying to extrapolate figures from prospectuses, wringing the last groat of information out of whatever data. Furthermore, I'm a model employee.'

She looked out of the window, fascinated by a telephone box.

Suddenly I could really *hear* myself. The man who spun a web of gold thread with his achievements and moved in for the kill when his intended was impressed.

Something's wrong with me – I almost said aloud.

Because I was trapped in a steel and glass temple to the twentieth-century religion – ambition, where I sat be-suited, be-cologned and be-haved at a chrome desk on the forty-second floor, staring into the glare of an electronic monitor, extracting facts and figures, which is what I would do for the rest of my working life. How long was that? Oh, only about another thirty years (by which time I'd be grey, wrinkled, arthritic, hunch-banked, pot-bellied, be-spectacled and deeply bitter). Oh, only about another 1,320 months (annual holidays already deducted). Oh, only about another 26,400 days (including bank holidays). Oh, only about another 72,000 hours (including breaks but excluding visits to the loo). Oh, only about another 1,320,000 minutes (of which roughly 50 per cent would be spent day-dreaming). Oh, only about another (I didn't get a First *fer nuttin'*) 79,200,000 seconds. And let's not go there with nanoseconds.

I had a vision of myself on Blackfriars Bridge, in the dead of night, swaying from a girder.

I shook my head and tutted like the tip-tip-tip of the high hat, trying to get Jessie's attention.

'Well, it's not to be sniffed at. I'm one of the few people in the world who know a lot about quantitative analysis.'

She slowly turned back, refocused her eyes and smiled indulgently.

'My, my, we're quite the chatterbox, aren't we? I get it – you were the school creep and now you're the office nerd.'

My upset showed. She laughed it off. 'Only kidding. I'm a joker, remember. That's why you were meant to meet me. Someone who can take you up to the high dive and say "Jump!"'

'Except we've just met,' I replied, shrugging, intrigued and flattered that anyone thought I'd even climb the high dive, let alone jump off.

'Sometimes you just know. Look, we click, don't we? I'm not asking you to marry me. Just come on an adventure. It's less fun on your own.'

'It's true. I've not felt so comfortable with anyone in ages, in fact, not ever.'

It wasn't true.

My mother.

Sometimes I thought I could sense her.

'Think of me as your fairy godmother, Stanley.'

Summer evenings, my mother and I used to sit snuggled up on the settee, drinking home-made sarsaparilla and watching a film or documentary, free to discuss anything and everything, but always within the framework of watching the box. We didn't even have to look at each other.

It was our way of communicating. Winters, we'd sip bush tea. Weekdays, my father was at the Working Men's Club. Weekends, he stayed in. Weekends, I went out.

It had been so many years since. And still, it was only now, this blustery seaside morning, that I could bear to recall how much I missed our evenings together. A time when I was simply adored for simply being myself. In the archive where I stored my mother, the settee-file was always the first to show itself, a succession of colour snapshops and snippets of conversation. I'm all bony angles and she's all squashy padding. I always put it right back on the shelf out of sight. Her fading away. Our farewells. The insufferable years afterwards. The solitude around me. The turbulence inside me. Still.

To this day. The terrible absence. And now. And then. This blustery seaside morning. Here. A woman was choosing my company. The first woman since who. And. She was. Yes. She was filling me up.

I leaned over to kiss Jessie, running my fingers gently down her throat, feeling her in the pit of my stomach as she responded. We ignored the pointed coughing from the till behind.

'Chemistry,' she said with surprising tenderness when she resurfaced. 'You know it'll be great even before you've done the doings. Then you look at the package and decide if you're prepared to buy into it. 'Course when you're younger you go for the package first and hope for the chemistry. Wait a minute, I think I've just swallowed one of your baked beans. It definitely wasn't mine. Anyroad, chemistry. When you get to my age, there's no does he or doesn't he. You just know.'

'Maybe you can teach me something.' I patted my lap, felt the warm squoodge of her buttocks strain my legs.

'Plural, actually,' she whispered in my ear, sending a shiver down my spine. 'If I didn't have a trick or two up my sleeve, I should be shot.'

'So long as I'm doing the shooting, that's all right.'

'I'm sure you've had lots of target practice, Action Man.'

'Yes, no, I mean, I have to tell you. I'm not very, well, like Don Juan or anything, well, I mean, like, thingy Travolta, or that, I'm not . . .'

I wanted to kick myself under the table. What an imbecile!

'What a sweetheart!' She pinched my cheeks, stroked my prickly overnight stubble. 'If you've not been up to the job so far, it's because your little girlfriends haven't been up to you. I'm here now.'

She wriggled like a coquette on my lap, making me rise. Jesus Christ, she was clenching me between her powerful cheeks.

I closed my eyes. When did I last sleep with a woman? My father was alive, so it was well over a year ago. Question: What happened after periods of abstinence? Answer: Premature ejac . . . I'd stain my trouse . . . Damn!

I quickly threw a bucket of cold water on the conversation.

'Tell me, Jessie, why not fly to Spain or Australia or wherever? It's quicker, safer, more ... sensible.' I sounded ridiculously interrogative.

'Am I hearing this?'

She sprang up, causing the crockery to shudder and almost sending me into a back flip.

'Come on, young man, let's deal with the elements. That's what we're here for – the air!'

She ran along the esplanade, laughing like a mad woman, and down the vertiginous concrete steps to the wide, empty beach in front of us. I hurried after her, trying to find sure footing on the slippery pebbles as she made for the promenade in the distance. She was behaving as I had always wanted to: charging along a beach like a child and whooping with joy, instead of shuffling along and worrying what people would think if I did.

'Sensible is a dirty word to me,' she said breathlessly, when I caught up. 'You're missing the point, which is to sample the freeway. What do you see stuck in a plane? Clouds! Thousands of miles in a few hours. *Not* natural.'

'But convenient,' I countered.

She slowed down. We walked together, heads bowed into a stirring wind that demanded respect, or else we'd be airborne to Calais. The sea air was affecting the tenor of our conversation. I could feel something being released.

'If you're in a hurry, but I won't be. I loved touring, even though some of the B & Bs were of a kind where the landladies turned the sheets over in between guests, a toilet brush was likely to be caked with brown bits or your mug of tea in the morning was stained with someone else's lipstick. We all loved Lily's Guest House on the edge of the Yorkshire moors. Put your photo into the silver frame on the piano just before you were due to arrive.'

We had reached the promenade, home to two iron benches bolted to the walls of a weather-beaten, planked-off caff. I faced the sea, felt my lungs expand.

'Go on, let it out,' she urged me. 'Scream – I am free! I am free! I am free!'

Down in the water, fishing boats banged against each other with a sound like the soft pads of African drums, building to a ritualistic crescendo against the wooden stakes of the pier.

I tried to scream but ended up choking. After all, if anyone had been around they would stare, and, although they'd be strangers I'd never see again, that was enough to stop me.

Still, I tried again and yelped like a dying sheepdog run over by a speeding truck. On the third attempt she joined me and I rode on her volume, then matched it and finally surpassed it. It was a pure Stanley Moment. One I will never forget. It had taken thirty-four years, nine months, three weeks and, yes, four days.

When the wind began to sprinkle spit on to our faces, we headed back towards the car. I'd lost almost a stone, well, about twelve pounds to be more precise.

'I've never stayed in a B & B,' I said, getting into the passenger seat, rubbing my hands together. 'Only in hotels as part of package holidays, Tenerife, Lanzarote, Jamaica, but that was with family, West Berlin once and –'

'Germany?' she cut in. 'I toured British Army bases in Germany once in my car. Those farmers trim their fields with nail scissors. Bavaria was like driving on to the set of *The Sound of Music*. Any moment you expected Julie Andrews to come dancing over a hill with a guitar in one hand and a load of blonde Heidis skipping behind her.'

'*The Sound of Music* was set in Austria, not Germany,' I corrected, seeing my breath cloud in front of me. 'The whole point was that Austria was under Nazi occupation.'

Facts were facts and fiction was fiction and never the twain should meet. I suspected they were often intertwined for Jessie O'Donnell.

She vigorously wiped the windscreen, which had steamed up with condensation.

'Don't be so pedantic, Stanley.'

I arched an eyebrow and gave her my 'mildly confrontational' look. She ignored it and revved the engine really loudly again.

'As I was saying, the recruits would swarm all over me after my act, even though back home I knew that a good few of them were of the kind to go "Paki-bashing".'

'That's just it. It's dangerous for us driving across Europe.' I was delighted to present an argument that carried weight. 'It's not safe for us out there. You only need to read the papers. Aborigines dying in police custody . . . Fascist thugs all over Europe . . . apartheid in South Africa . . .'

'Excuses, poor excuses. Stop acting like a resident without a permit.'

We were driving up the high street to pick up the main road out of Broadstairs. Morning was starting to happen: Tesco's shutters were being pulled up. Schoolgirls and boys were joshing around at a bus stop. A long-haired man was pruning plants that hung from lamp-posts. Workmen were starting to drill in a side road. The school-run was slowing down traffic.

'My father always said I was a Jamaican first and foremost.'

It had always been a statement, but now I imagined a question mark on the end. What did I, Stanley Orville Cleve Williams, think?

I watched Jessie fire up, assuming the authoritative tone of a statesman about to deliver a sermon to a junior. She reminded me of my father, clearing his throat to remonstrate with the young son who had yet to learn that he could not contradict this elder on any matter.

'You're just another Englishman, don't kid yourself. You think like an Englishman, walk like an Englishman, talk like an English-man, eat like an Englishman and most likely you dance like an Englishman. You've spent all your life in England, Stanley, so what does that make you? Mongolian? Peruvian? Egyptian?'

Did it make sense? Maybe. But I wasn't going to be crushed like a can of Coke.

'I don't have any real roots here. None of us has.'

Was I really just like him, hanging on to a state of statelessness? *We don't belong, Stanley.* So why did he never make it back home, where presumably he did belong?

'Think you'll find, Stanley, that slavery and the colonies were a pipeline of liquid fertilizer pumping away into the British soil for four hundred years so that the money trees on this fair isle could grow big and strong. Think that gives us land rights, don't you? Look, the point is to be always on the move. How exciting is that?'

'A bit too exciting for me,' I replied. 'I like going home to the same bed, I think. Everyone does, don't they?'

'If you haven't tried it, how do you know? Tell me, when did you last take a risk?'

The only risks I'd ever taken had been calculated and financial. I said nothing.

'How are you going to grow if you never take risks? Look, you could wait a year or you could do it now and really test your mettle. Life's far too extraordinary ever to offer guarantees because if you can predict what's around the corner, then you're merely surviving, not truly living.'

'I've always known what's around the corner.' I tried to take back my words but they went on regardless. 'Then my father died and now it seems – my dreams were his.'

'I'm sorry to hear that. When did he die?'

Jessie sounded like a counsellor, infused with professional concern. No, it was genuine. Well, if she could say 'I don't need any pity, love', then so could I.

'A year ago.'

'Tell me about him.'

'I'd rather not, at least not yet.'

Full stop. End of errand.

She stroked my cheek with the back of her hand. I wanted to cry. 'When you're ready.'

She was right. I'd shut out all possibilities so that nothing had surprised me until my father's death, which I couldn't avoid. I could hand in my notice, rent out my flat to a friend. What was keeping me here? School report, 1988: STANLEY IS FREE. Gold Medal of Exceptional Bravery.

'Yes, it was all to please my father.'

Now he's gone. It's scary.

'What have you got to lose?'

'My career?'

Even as I spoke, I knew the argument against it.

'What have you got to gain?'

'Living in the world instead of watching it spin by.'

'That's right and you go, come back, pick up where you left off, wiser, more fulfilled, more worldly. I mean, what do you want on your gravestone? STANLEY PAID HIS MORTGAGE ON TIME AND WAS NEVER LATE FOR WORK. THE BANKING INDUSTRY WILL SORELY MISS HIM.'

'What if we don't get on?' I ventured, watching her.

'I'll make sure we get on.' She said it with such a lack of hesitation that I guessed she'd have enough determination to make things work for both us.

It was tempting. It was crazy. Yesterday I was trapped. Today I felt reckless.

'I don't know!'

'Stop thinking so much and act.'

'I'm confused!'

'Then I'm getting through to you. I'm on the long road to nowhere in this place. I want to be out *there*.' Jessie laughed bitterly. 'Some would say I already am.'

'I don't think you are. I think you're absolutely amazing.'

She let the compliment wash over her. Maybe she couldn't take it. Maybe she wasn't as self-assured as she appeared. Mum used to say that some people had strong personalities but were of weak character – and the two shouldn't be confused.

'I'm leaving soon, very soon. If it doesn't work out, there's always the little sparrow Edith Piaf to fall back on.'

She belted out a passionately poor imitation of Piaf: '*No. No regrets . . .*'

'Shame I've got to keep my eye on the road or else I'd be . . .'

She slid a hand between my thighs, up to my crotch, unzipped my flies, squeezed and rubbed as I opened my legs wider and let out a gratified groan.

She moved the car smoothly into fourth.

Pilgrimage, of sorts, to see my little buddha,
living low beneath my belly in Australia.

Going to trundle over that pregnant swell of earth
and drop in on your family in Sydney, Terry.

Don't want to go by air, all pie in the sky,
best go by road, prepare for both kinds of welcome.

I was choking mad, you were going to leave.
I did what no mother should have to remember.

Can you hear me, Terry, forgive me, Terry?
Oh, the sight, stench and sizzle of frazzled skin,

the way smoke rose off it, your gasp, my scream,
your punishment, my penance, your disappearance.

19 words last Christmas, not a cheap card neither,
but no *love from*, no *come and visit*, no symbolic kiss.

A good wife, you said, first-born child, you said,
twelve years after I'd given you up for dead . . .

Clerken-well

Jessie's room was the cheapest that she could find, and, while she had scrubbed it down upon arrival, it still smelled of must from the wet walls and the withered royal blue carpet, its squillion gold stars made dull with age. It said impermanence – that the person residing within could pack up and leave within the hour.

The room was just wide enough for a lumpy double futon, at the end of which a wrinkled wardrobe stood like a retired Sumo wrestler ready to keel over. Sellotaped on to the scuffed wall was a large map of the world, faded white at its fold lines. Upon it, a black marker pen had shot a wide-arching arrow from London all the way down to Australia.

J An orange glow moves up from my toes, spreading inside me. Sometimes you just *know*

S I slip off her diaphanous negligee. Oh – my – goddess.

J Devouring me with those eyes of his. Makes me feel deliciously *wanton*

S She's so, shall we say, Pre-Raphaelite, only darker, and with much larger breasts (42EE?)

J Stronger than he looks, but not so's I couldn't pin him down

S Such chewable lips that seek mine. Such billowy arms embracing mine

J His hands are so sensitive, like radar. Finding my magic spot, heating it up

S My hands warm her breasts. The cup runneth over

J Come and drink your milk-ilicious, Baby-Boy

S Not skimmed, semi-skimmed or fat-free but full-bodied whole: a mouth-watering, lactating fantasy

J It's long but not as lean as his feet would suggest. In girth, more like bratwurst than chipolata, thankfully. Whatever they say – it *does* matter

S I'm lying weightless on top of a water bed

J My fingers count each vertebrae down to his coccyx, then circle and . . .

S I've never allowed *that* before. It's quite . . . Oooh . . .

J If only I had a strap-on

S No jutting-out bones to scrape against mine like hammers and chisels in a tool bag

J Would he let me? Would he?

S Smells of sweat. Tastes of toothpaste. Damn! I forgot to brush mine

J Don't mind his manky-breath at all. I must be smitten, eh?

S I venture downstairs. The bathroom is so clean and, well, nice-smelling

J As I moan I see us driving down the autobahn at 150mph, whooping it up, deliriously

S I clamber back up. A job well done. There's pleasure in pleasuring another

J Ten out of ten, my tail-wagging puppy dog

S Now I'm trying to navigate, but you know, sometimes . . . a guy fumbles

J Let me get you an *A–Z*, dear. Or should we join the local orienteering society? How about a compass?

S I did tell you I wasn't Don Juan

J Never mind, I'll be your Girl Guide. Arkala!

S She's saluting. She's cracking me up!

J We-Will-Do-Our-Best!

S I want sweet nothings, but all I can manage is *You're really turning me on*

J Which is nothing short of unimaginative, Stanley

S When I'm inside her, shall we say, tropical lushness, I feel so . . . male

J When he's inside me, I want to pull up the drawbridge and bolt it

S Wanted comfort (100%). Wanted contrast (100%). Wanted to come (100%)

J Come with me, Stanley, dear. Wake up to wide open fields and driving on a road that leads up and away into the heavens

S She opens her eyes and a tear escapes, which she quickly wipes away

J He's grinning like a teenager what's just lost his virginity

S We've found each other, Miss O'Donnell

J Yes, we have, Mr Williams

S She rolls on top of me and I completely disappear

J Dissolve into me, for eternity . . .

Thus did the early morning find them, a cubist painting, Stanley imagined, of two newly formed lovers, unclothed bodies divided into segments of browns, the geometry of dismembered planes.

One of his thighs placed at right angles over a cylindrical calf, his stomach a bronze disc, perfectly knotted navel at his hub, her conical breast eclipsed by a disembodied hand.

Her plaits swept into a fan of black spokes, to startling effect on the white sheet, as if an artist had laid them out that way, so peacefully, so symmetrically.

As we lay watching Jessie sleep, she opened her eyes and looked up at the ceiling.

'William,' she said, her voice eerie, strangely olde-worlde.

Now who in God's name was William, Stanley wondered. One of Jessie's exs? He wasn't used to these jolts. He was used to predicting his emotional journey through any given day, yes, like a good old Roman road. Since he'd met Jessie he'd already been up the Himalayas and through the Khyber Pass. What next? White-water rafting in Jamaica?

Stanley sat up and watched as Jessie climbed over the mattress, seemingly without the weight of bone, muscle, organ or water, a sleepwalker with a fulness of purpose. Reaching the window, she gravitated towards the shadows, where she appeared to morph into someone else:

A certain Lucy Negro, standing
in her tumbledown lodgings in Clerken-well,

looking down at the hawkers and dummerers
whom she knows only too well,

like Eileen 'Evil Eye' Wilson, applying ratsbane
on to her corpulent chest and flaccid arms,

the better to raise odious sores,
the better to make herself a pitiful beggar,

Lucy's *madam* when she first arrived in the city.
There go the pottle-pot and vintner boys –

Grocer Markham's grandson Arthure,
barrel perched atop his head, back sunk low

over speeding, ricket-bowed legs.
Young Eddie, Widow Sexton's slave boy,

two caskets in outstretched arms, told
to run faster than a whipped horse

and barely seven years old at that.
There goes slithering Lord Etherington,

sniffing out the alleyway skirts he lifts weekly,
nose so lofty he steps first into a dark

coil of dog's shit, then a paler, colder porridge
of human excrement, whereupon he ends

up squashed in a goodly dollop of both,
creasing the whole street up with mirth,

a whole street's worth of sneering, sore-addled lips,
a whole street's worth of gunge-curdled teeth.

And there the purveyors of the oldest trade,
Maude, Mags, Polly, Kat, Thomasina,

Lucy's colleagues all and on frequent occasions
her opponents in spectacular cat fights,

mucus entangled in fistfuls of flying hair,
which she is always odds-on favourite to win.

There, down stage right, stands Lucy,
looking down on life, as she knows it.

Lucy with her blazing face. Her defiant equestrian neck. Her swaying, working girl's hips. She is squeezed into a theatrical replica of
a gentlewoman's attire, which makes her look like a moulting
peacock. Cream boned bodice with pasteboard stomacher, quince-
yellow ribbons threaded through. A green and purple ruffled skirt
with a wheel farthingale inside that makes getting through door-
ways difficult. Voluminous puffed sleeves, fringed with lace, are
dusty and fragile as spiders' webs.

Dry and brittle coconut husk head
braided into cane rows
worked up towards a knotted plait at her crown.

Two clan scars float delicately
down her cheekbone,
like the sapling blades of a paradise palm.

Lucy is distinguished from all the other working girls in no greater
way than the exquisite design on her back.

A circle of cicratice dots
stamped betwixt shoulder blades,
like a disc of sunflower florets.

An alphabet for clients
to decipher with dumbstruck hands,
as if it holds the secret to her.

A wonderful new hieroglyphics
from the African world over the oceans
only seafaring men can imagine.

Another time. Another place. Another people. Perhaps not fully
human at all.

But Lucy has no time for the sentimental longings of an African
Albion. Her home over Jordan. Her Jerusalem.

She cannot remember much about her village on the Guinea
coast, or the ship *Jesus of Lübeck* that brought her west in 1563; but
she will never forget Lady Margaret Measse of Linton in Yorkshire,
who purchased Lucy precisely so she could set her newly freed
charge on the villainous, boggy road to London, with enough
shillings to pay for inns and coaches and enough money to last a
year when she arrived. Not enough for a lifetime, though.

Harlot! Doxy! Meretrix! Lucy Negro, who used to trade outside
the Swan, a beershop in Turnbull Street.

A straw pallet is slumped against the wall in the far-right corner of the room. It is like a disgruntled innkeeper with rolls of overlapping fat who has fallen asleep drunk, having discharged semen into her. It has a coverlet of dogswain and a dirty grey bolster at the head. A gentleman's black cloak is flung upon it.

Lucy bites her bottom lip, wincing when she feels the scab. A warrant from the Queene was recently posted on the streets.

> Her Majestie understanding that there are of late divers blackamoores brought into this realme, of which kinde there are all ready here to manie . . .
>
> Her Majesty's pleasure therefore ys that those kinde of people should be sent forth of the lande . . .

The soldiers will hunt her down. This is worse than her worst nightmare: the torture of pilliwinks upon her fingers, the accusation Witch!

She is not alone. Centre stage. William.

A well-known playwright and bit-part thespian, William sits on a three-legged stool, looking slavishly up at Lucy. His features are like many another dreamy-eyed poet's: tallow-complexioned, strong nose, sensitive lips, the makings of a beard and moustache. He wears a black velvet doublet with gold trim, black breeches cut into cerise silk panels and fashionably slashed leather shoes with cork heels. In his right hand are several sheets of foul papers, drafts of some love poems.

Oh, and he stinks. They all do. Stanley finds himself gagging as he peers over William's shoulder and dips into his heart and mind, this newly discovered ability seemingly the most natural thing in the world.

Winter mist has been creeping up on William ever since his young son Hamnet died:

> Grief fills the room up of my absent child

Grief comes in waves, he has learned. Too often his tears are so swilled that their sediment, anger, rises to the surface, leaving the taste of bitterness stinging his throat. No one understands him. He is always having to prove himself. Because he is the son of an illiterate glove-maker. The upstart playwright who didn't go to university. Because the woman he loves is a bloody strumpet who, after all these years, still makes him feel like a man naked in a forest in a thunderstorm.

He is unravelling his papers. They are not yet published and he wants to test them on his current *objet d'amour*. Stanley looks down at the parchment paper, the jagged handwriting in black ink, the crossings out and thumb smudges, and realizes it's written in Elizabethan English and he can scant comprehend it.

William: My love is as a fever, longing still,
   For that which longer nurseth the disease.

He recites like an actor, typically over-egging his vowels and attacking consonants with an excess of plosive gusto. Lucy replies in a rotten English, cobbled together from the gutter and the gentry.

Lucy: William, thou art such a wimp. Pull thyself together.
  I am in a mire and only thee can extricate me.

William reads from another sonnet, but Stanley finds himself fixated on Lucy. Her presence so dominates the room that he cannot help but be drawn to her, like someone else he has just met.

William: Past cure I am, now reason is past care,
   And frantic-mad with evermore unrest.

Lucy: Well, that makes two of us. Past care am I too,
  and frantic mad with terrible turbulence.

William: Thou art as tyrannous, so as thou art,
   As those whose beauties proudly make them cruel.

Lucy: Yea, yea, but I do have a problem, sirrrah!
  Marry! 'Tis not safe for my kinde here any more.

Her Majestie will have all blackamoores banished.
I will be as a fox with no place to hide. Damned

by the colour of my skin, hounded. As I speak,
they are rounding us up. I can no longer tarry.

William shuffles through his papers.

William: I will hound thee too, because of thy skin.
Listen to this verse. 'Tis the best ever written.

'My mistress's eyes are nothing like the sun;
Coral is far more red than her lips' red;

If snow be white, why then her breasts are dun;
If hairs be wires, black wires grow on her head.'

Lucy: S'truth, give me metal, William! I beseech thee.
Use thy sway with your patron, Henry,

Earl of Southampton, to have me ensconced
within a castle until this terror subsides.

Now listen to me and stop droning on with your
romantic folly. I have heard it all afore

from countless men who grace my bed
and bugger off without even a *ta ra, then,*

forgetting their fine gentlemanly manners,
that I, a lowly pro, have feelings too.

[Aside] Or did have once, when I was wild and green
and transplanted from wild forest and beach

and heat and sea and a spoken tongue
as soft on the ears as sand granules running

through mine fingers. Until I came to this,
this machiavellian city of stinking deceit.

William: Fie! Thou art too froward, woman.
Thou wilt be safe here. Worry not.

Canst thou not see that thou hath inspired
greatness in me? Now, listen to this one.

'Therefore my mistress's eyes are raven black,
Her brow so suited, and they mourners seem
At such, who, not born fair, no beauty lack,
Sland'ring creation with false esteem:
Yet so they mourn, becoming of their woe,
That every tongue says, beauty should not look so.'

William's gaze shifts to the window, where he dreams upon the miracle of his own poetry. His words sound familiar to Stanley, but he cannot quite put his finger on it. He is mindful to nudge William and tell him to climb back down from his own fundament and listen to what this Lucy-woman is telling him. He must take her away from the city, which is closing in on her. Stanley wonders if he is also convincing himself.

William: So oft have I invok'd thee for my Muse,
And found such fair assistance in my verse.

Lucy: Then stop the drivel and help me out, goddamit!

She prowls around William like a big cat sizing up its prey. Stanley hopes she'll bend over William so that her breasts pop up from her bodice and squash against his own back. William thinks he will never understand women, but knows enough to allow them to let off steam every now and then, like Annie, back home in Stratford.

Lucy: Even though I'm just an image for thy poems
Merely a play on darkness against the light

or somesuch nonsense for them to quibble over.
O, and a great fuck too!

William tries to grab her, but she swings out of his reach.

William: To win me soon to hell my female end.

Lucy: Yes, twisted, and rotting and worse than a snake's bite.
        And thou knowst what? Everyone's had me!

Lucy sinks to her knees before William, resting her head on his lap.

But truly I am so afeared and only thou can help.
Even Mistress Widdecombe downstairs

who owns this lodgings will turn me out.
She hates my trade in men, though she loves

the rub of coins in her sweaty palm more.
Dost thou know that she rivals the puritanical

Lizbet as the oldest virgin in all of England?
Indeed she is so proud of it she will tell

anyone who cares to listen of her purity.
Why, methinks she will lift her skirts

and show us her pitted old apricot any minute.
She *will* turn me out, though, William.

These past few days I have seen the gleam
of bleating victory in her froggy eyes.

William: I love it when you're vicious, Lucy dear.

Stanley cups her face in his hands. She rolls her eyes, tries to pull
back, but his fierce second sight holds her fast. Her eyes widen as
if she knows William has been inhabited, and she herself too. It is
Jessie who is staring up with such passion, with such longing. It
is Jessie who is seeking her own escape, who is offering Stanley
the keys to the kingdom of freedom.

Lucy: Don't mourn for me when I am dead, William,
        when you hear the sullen bell ring out,

        warning the world that your beloved has fled
        from this vile world, with viler worms to cohabit.

William: Well thou know'st, to my dear-doting heart
        Thou art the fairest and most precious jewel.

William leans towards her, closes his eyes and pouts his lips.

William: Kissy kissy, my lovely?

Lucy: In truth, thou hast no idea, spoilt Wills.
        My hell art thine heaven. Blessed be thee.

Rising to her feet in exasperation, Lucy leads him towards the bed.
William follows, a mischievous smile on her behind.

William: Wench!

Stanley: What the hell was . . .

Jessie: What's the matter?

Stanley sat upright on the mattress like a marionette being yanked
up at the forehead by its puppet master's strings. Jessie awoke
sensuously beside him, placed her palm on to his lower back and
curled into him with the suppleness of a cat.

'Come back to sleep: it's still only Saturday, you don't have to
work today, sweetie.'

Her cheeks were smooth as caramel. He wanted to lick them, to
stroke them. No scars, no stench. She turned away, but Stanley
wanted more.

He was sure he could see a rash of mosquito bites between her
shoulder blades, but when he reached over they dissolved under
the light touch of his fingers. Jessie could take him places, he
decided.

I dreamt another world, magicked into this one.
Lingering at the tail-end of the twentieth,
yet mauling the rotten gut of the sixteenth.

Was it all true and how did Lucy Negro die?
Shall I compare thee to a summer's day?
Thou art so right, dear, somnolent Jessie.

It's quickly coming back, memory's been jolted:
Virgin Queen, Stonehenge, Tower of London,
all dumped when strong-armed into sciences.

My classmates mucked around on the coach ride home.
But I carried it all with me: beheaded wives, Druids,
battles re-enacted in those dreary autumn skies.

Though no one resembled me – until now.
Somewhere, out there, in this great unknown ether.
This history, this country – could it really be mine?

'I'm going to travel with you,' Stanley whispered, as he snuggled down beside Jessie, wrapping her up in his arms.

   'You already have done,' came the reply, but by then he too had fallen asleep.

Grief fills up the room of my absent father.
Took leave of absence in his last years,
the woman he belonged to – gone.
He felt he never, ever belonged – here

was black Lucy in Elizabeth's England
a dream witnessed by your son
whose dreams had been deferred
in deference to you – Father?

I could smell her terrible breath, so close,
touch coarse hair, woven
like Pearline's in parched photographs,
no pomade to soften, then, softening

your passing for there is more of life
in death than I supposed. Father,
I have found a fiery woman of whom
you would not approve, desperate

to escape, as you could not escape
yourself, and stirring all around
are whispers, winds, are ethereal beings,
who might just make me whole.

Stanley decided to do some research, a rather pretentious term, he admitted, for such amateurish rooting about in the library. When he discovered that a Lucy Negro really had existed in six-teenth-century London and that she used to trade outside the Swan in Turnbull Street, he sat down at the rectangular communal desk replete with the day's newspapers, scribbling students and tramps pretending not to fall asleep, where he moved a combination of faith, fact and disbelief back and forth in his mind, like a game of high-speed table tennis.

Fifty-one Days in Blackheath

S   beef casserole with black lingerie
           lipstick warhols my cheeks
           welcome home, banker-boy

J   marinating Stanley
           massage flank, shank (spank)
           and oh that feather-less chest

S   on the 6th day, a scummy bath
           j'accustory finger – suctioned off
           late for work (a first)

J   hootchy-kootchy, cha-cha, boogaloo
           each touch leads to double-shuffle
           bathroom, sitting room, bog (bed)

S   dramatics of a prima donna
           when your father dies
           your needs become primal again

J   cache of champagne
tomorrow is today for Crissakes
let's celebrate (virgin crystal flutes)

S   puddle of crumpled clothes
I crush silk panties
inhale indecent scent

J   filing boxes under bed
bills, bank statements, investments
not really prying, just investigating

S   *Dynasty* versus Jacques Cousteau
she sits on remote control
tickle, relinquish, conquest

J   he requested night alone
dialled my digits at midnight
taxi-take, receipt-keep

S   mating on Blackheath common
      criss-cross roads, searchlight car beams
      lord, my merry days!

J   day 46 – wine on white sofa
      just like menstrual spots
      rushed to salt it up, *don't worry* (me, speechless)

S   skin of sun-drenched petals
      enfolds me at dark
      releases me at dawn

J   someone to talk to
      someone who listens
      someone who remembers what I've said

S   glass silence shattered
      empty space decorated
      with glowing psychedelic strokes

London Au Revoir

Matilda piled on the pounds at Calais: food, petrol and gallons of expectation. She then dragged her newly obese self on to the autoroute, fidgeting about in the back until the dried goods and perishables settled into each other's paper-bag grooves.

It was a long list of firsts for Stanley, he told Jessie repeatedly.

'First time handing in my notice. First time renting out my flat. First time going abroad: destination unknown / duration indeterminate. First time entering the lock-jawed mouth of a ferry. First time towing a caravan (circa 1970), which, I must say, could easily fly off into a field and end up crashed into a tree or upside down in a ditch and then we'd be homeless if not with broken spines or even dead!'

'Stop mithering me,' Jessie said, sighing. 'Know what I'm doing.'

'But I'm not sure that I do.' He looked at her, then at the door, as if contemplating getting out.

'You're not going to let me down, are you, love?' There was alarm in her voice. 'I'm depending on you. So long as you're with me, you're all right.'

'Stop the car,' he said. 'Please!'

She did so and the car jolted to an abrupt halt.

'We don't even have a guide book or a proper road map.' Stanley's voice was hoarse.

'To some people, spontaneity is a dirty word, but it's my modus operandi. See, you're not the only one with a fancy vocab. There's a lot to be learned at the University of HK, Hard Knocks. I've got a degree too, in Life – Life's Shitty Experiences. Only got a third, though. Third-degree burns.'

'But why make things difficult for ourselves when we can plan out the route and choose the best campsites in advance?'

'Properly is a dirty word to me, Stanley. Do you think the Bushmen of the Kalahari need a list of "Best Trees to Sleep Under"? Did that prophet Jesus need the *Rough Guide to the Desert* when he went out to fast, and a list of "Things to Do and See" when he got bored? Did early African man need the *Lonely Planet Guide to Evolution* in order to reach Norway? And, trust me, it was lonely, walking with the future of humanity on your hairy shoulders. No, they did not. They used that underrated asset called instinct, coupled with past knowledge and general wherewithal. It's what's in our genes that will get us to our destination.'

'Which is?' he asked with impatience.

'Spain, as you well know.'

'And thereafter?'

'When we're ready, we'll move eastwards.'

'But it still doesn't make sense. We're just making things more difficult for ourselves.'

Jessie exploded. 'Will you shut the fuck up, Mr Whingealot! This is supposed to be a freewheeling adventure, not an expedition planned with military precision.'

Stanley giggled, then went quiet for a few moments before pointing suspiciously at Matilda's bonnet. 'Anyway, how do I know she hasn't got intestinal cancer or some other disease?'

'Matilda is Russian. *Comprenez?* Which means she was built to withstand those freeze-your-bollocks-off Siberian winters. She throws a fit only if pushed too hard.'

'Better not push her too hard, then.' He glared at her.

To which she replied, 'I'm not the sort of person to rise to the bait.'

'But you have to have the last word,' he added, mumbling. 'Like someone else I used to know.'

'No, I don't, and what was that?'

'*Nuttin*.'

Stanley didn't want to be childish, but he couldn't help himself. He began ticking off a new list of concerns with his fingers.

'No return plane ticket. No insurance. No hotel reservation. No holiday rep with a smile and clipboard. No "Orientation Cocktails at 6 p.m. in the hotel bar".'

'No grumpy Monday-morning starts,' Jessie responded. 'No rush-hour stress. No incarceration in an office block. No worrying about what you've left behind, Stanley.'

'No, but lots of worrying about what lies ahead.'

'Look, we're turtles now. We'll find an empty campsite, I'll cook summat, then we'll turn off the lamp and wait for a gang of Neo-Nazis to jump out of the bushes and set fire to the caravan.'

Stanley burst out laughing.

'This is what I want to see. I need you with me completely, laddie. Not with your head back in London, worrying. Just relax and enjoy the adventure.' She patted his knee.

'I forgot to add, first time in love too.' He paused, grinning. 'With an older woman.'

'May I remind you, Mr Incipient Middle Age, that I'm not even old enough to be your mother? Same generation, so stop fantasizing, boyo!'

'Are you going to beat me for being naughty?'

Jessie cuffed him around the head. 'Get away with you. That's a treat for when you're being good.'

La France

Fresh grapes for popcorn –
my very own motion picture
not grainy monochrome but pastoral
with Dolby Surround Sound.

Never noticed birds at home
(club-foot pigeons).
Here, a gull, crow, there – sparrows.
I tune into Morse code.

Militaristic crew-cut,
hippie's dehydrated blonde,
acres of dark mossy armpits,
who'd have thought it, of grass.

What colour my office carpet?
Shade of brown my father's eyes?
My computer – black or grey?

Passing cities of outlaw forests
(brick does not grow),
a witch-doctor's whisk of horses,
a rabbit, flattened by the roadside.

Her hands are moths when talking.
She crotchets her plaits when excited.
She palms my knee at 80° Fahrenheit.
Let's freeze-frame/our first/on-screen/kiss (Indie).

The Freeway

Cattle herds and orchards. Lovely medieval towns of Normandy, but once you've seen one, you've seen them all: *boulangerie*; *charcuterie*; *whatooterie*.

'Look at the size of that tree!' Stanley pointed to a large oak.

'Yes, isn't it amazing how it's got a trunk and branches.'

Split his sides at that.

'Course if it doesn't work out, I'll be looking for the 666 sign burned into his scalp and yours truly will end up in Jessie's Inferno, yet again. Glad I've found him, for now, which is what matters, seeing as for ever's always a day away. Those tight little buns fit my hands perfectly. Nice to have a squeeze when I feel like it.

'Let's go to Versailles,' he said out of the blue, somewhat imploringly.

'Do you really want to? It'll bore the socks off you,' I said, trying to dissuade him.

'I'd love to. One of the French kings, right?'

'No, one of the Aztec ones. And *you're* the one with the degree. Louis XIV, to be precise. His idea of a country cottage, initially. We'll go in the morning.'

CAMPING was signposted from the road – the French word the same as the English. Still, Stanley kindly translated it for me. A long ride down a bumpy lane lined with poplars until we came to an unlocked gate. 'Actually, I do know some French,' I said. 'Although the only words I need to know in any language are *You started it!*'

He cranked down the caravan and I got cooking. Then he gathered firewood. 'Hey,' he said as it began to crackle. 'All my handiwork.'

There he was, jumping up and down, doing a little dance.

'Congratulations,' I chuckled. 'It's no mean feat rubbing two flints together, Cave Man.'

Chopped some onions and courgettes and fried them in a pan. He watched, fascinated.

'It's called cooking, and if you tell me you've never seen someone cook in the open air before, I'll clobber you.'

He swiped a slice of courgette, put it in his mouth and hopped off like a kangaroo. Have to pinch myself. He's *thirty-four*.

'Don't make a mess,' he said, picking up the peelings from the forest floor.

'Sorry. It's such a nice white carpet, isn't it? I should be more careful.'

'We should respect nature.'

'I'm respecting the insects' right to eat. Equal rights for all, that's what I say. You don't want those innocent little mites to starve, do you?'

He cleans up after me all the time, does Stanley. He's this picker-upper following me around and tidying up my so-called mess.

Jessie, if you leave stale food in the car it'll attract flies.

Jessie, this suitcase is for *your* clothes, and this one is for *mine*.

Jessie, don't put loose change on the dashboard because it just falls down.

Jessie, keep the bananas separate from the other fruit or they'll rot.

Jessie, please squeeze the toothpaste from the bottom.

Jessie, where have you put my pen, mug, trainers, socks, razor?

I just ignore him. He'll give up, eventually, and do things my way.

Tangled branches clasped each other beneath the dark sky. A rushing river in the distance. Movement of wings in the trees. Soft bed of leaves and twigs underneath our trainers. Both wearing trackies. Mine were dark blue with a silver stripe. His were light grey with a dark blue stripe. Got them in Olympus Sportswear, Oxford Street. My idea. Practical.

'Holidays were what other families did,' he said, staring into the burning bracken.

'Tell me about it.'

'Yes, you and me both.'

'No, I mean tell me about your family. What was it like to have one? What was it like to lose one?'

He shook his head and let the flames hypnotize him.

I poured some Armagnac into plastic beakers.

'Liquid gold,' I said, gulping it back in one swig.

And we'd lost the moment.

Threw a rosemary bush on to the fire. It filled the air with incense.
It was just me, him, our secrets, the fire, the night and good times
ahead . . .

'Thank you for bringing me here, Jessie. I feel so alive. I could
be here for ever.'

He looked up and we soaked up each other's appreciative gaze.

You and me both, I was tempted to agree.

Hall of Mirrors, Versailles

The Château de Versailles is one of the largest palaces the world has ever known, and it swallows its mass of visitors whole, without so much as a genteel burp. Upon entering the forecourt, Stanley's mouth released silent exclamation marks. Jessie's mouth clamped shut as she swept up the vista with a reluctant glance, then dumped it right back down again.

Wintertime, Versailles was often obscured beneath a mantle of snow; the only signs of life were puffs of charcoal emanating from the lodges on the outskirts. Summertime, the gardens erupted into orchestrated displays of technicolour, the paths besieged by tourists. This early spring invited a smaller clientele, the real business taking place underground, where pods passed through their fleeting teenage months, waiting for the cyclic sun to draw them out of themselves and into a rampant, flush-faced maturity.

I cruise above its panoramic grounds,
black nun's habit billowing . . .

Jessie and Stanley hooked fingers within the maze of gardens, which spun out geometrically around a main axis with radiating pathways, pools and arbors. Versailles, Stanley decided, with its two thousand windows, seven hundred rooms and two thousand acres of park, was simply the most spectacular place he had ever visited. And here he was, mid-week, mid-day, mid-life (almost), and, instead of staring listlessly out of his office menagerie, he was daring to align himself with the sky and follow the changing landscapes that spread beneath it.

I yearn for texture, scent, taste,
but feel nothing, not even my own fingers.

They passed the boxwood hedges of the Parterre du Midi, scattering robins and pigeons, then over to the Parterre du Nord, with its verdurous, striped lawns.

'Majestic surroundings can take one's mind off other preoccupations,' Stanley mused aloud. Such as a dying father, was his afterthought. Jessie met his wistful smile with stretched lips, whose spread northwards to the eyes was as impossible as scaling a sheer cliff without crampons.

> *I go for a dip, without getting wet,*
> *burrow into pungent earth*
>
> *where pineapple once grew,*
> *recalling the time when I had to eat.*
>
> *I lift myself over espaliered trees*
> *and sail through lofty walls.*

Stanley did not see the dark nun glissade down the slope beneath the palace, but, out of the corner of his eye, he imagined he saw a large black bird descend with extended wings.

> *It is where I like to dream*
> *of Mother and the African dwarf Nabo –*
> *rumour had it, he was my father.*

In the Orangery, there were paths lined with the perfectly snipped Afros of hundreds of small orange trees. Like a line-up of Motown singers in repose, Stanley said to Jessie, who appeared not to hear him.

They entered the Grand Apartment, its seven rooms dedicated to the seven planets. The Room of Abundance, where coffee and liqueurs had been served. The Mercury Room, which had once been brimming with gaming and music. Stanley tried to envisage the aristocrats, courtiers and hangers-on, those whose bearing would acquire a new dignity upon entering a residence that surely demanded expansion of its swanning classes, and considerable athletic stamina from its serving classes.

He found his back stiffening, legs gliding. An imperious expression flitted across his face. Jessie was the queen at his side. Or should have been.

But here in this monument to grandiosity and pomposity, hunched forward in a navy-blue windcheater, the spring had broken in her feet. She would never be revered. Or glorified. Or mythologized. Billie Holiday. Edith Piaf. Bessie Smith. Not.

She wanted Stanley to notice her mood.

Great houses reminded her of St Ann's Children's Home, the Victorian mansion high up in the hills of Leeds run by the Sisters of Mercy, whose greater love was for God but with a generic love for all mankind. She remembered the do-gooders whose smiles were undisguised vehicles of condescension and pity, the prospective parents who would pat her head, marvel at the bounce of her hair, but never chose to take her home, to love her, unconditionally.

No one understood. Not Stanley. Not no one. And no one ever would.

Royal histories with their centuries-old family trees reminded her that hers possessed three names: an irresponsible absconder, an abandoned orphan and one adored son, Terry – who left a dash after his name, and the acidic after-taste of his parting words: *If you insist on an explanation, Mum, I have to be my own person, which means I have to get away from you!* Spat out when he was sixteen and changing shoe size three times a year. She tried to stop him leaving the kitchen, her back to the door, hands gripping the knob so tightly it would have snapped off, if she hadn't been dripping with sweat. Then she lost control . . .

It was only when Jessie snatched herself away from Stanley with a look of irritation that it dawned on him that theirs was not the companionable silence of two people who do not feel forced to make small talk. Rather, it stretched between them like an elastic band, ready to snap and ping in his face. He decided to break it.

'This is the first time I've ever –'

'Don't!'

'Don't what?'

'Just don't say this is the first anything ever again.'

He stared at Jessie's scowling face. 'But this is Versailles. I've never seen anything like it before.'

'Shows us how the other half lives, that's for sure.'

'Jessie, no one lives like this now.'

'Whatever. Look, I can't do this any more . . .'

'What do you mean, you can't do this? This is supposed to be pleasure, not penance. Isn't this what it's all about – seeing the sights?'

'Not for me it isn't. I'm not interested in dead things or touristic things like great big fuck-off Rococo palaces.'

'Well, I wish you'd told me.'

'Meaning?'

'I love seeing the sights.'

She started backing away. 'And I love drinking tea, so I'm going for one, or, more likely, *une tasse de thé*, if they've got it. You coming?'

The invitation was a gauntlet thrown down on the floor. Her expression was indiscernible as the sun blocked it out, leaving her in shadow.

She shrugged. 'You'll find me in the café when you're done. Don't worry about little old me.'

Gobsmacked, he watched her turn and storm off, long canvas bag hugging her hips, plaits jumping up and down as she shook her head. He noticed the prowl of her shoulders, the way she kicked up the pebble path, suggesting the countdown to a detonation. No, thanks. He wouldn't chase after her. He hadn't come here to sit in a café. He could do that in Blackheath Village. They'll talk later. Right now all he wanted to do was return to the seventeenth century.

A few inches above the ground,
I trail him, sensing he is susceptible.

His trainers squeaking on seventy-three metres of polished parquet floor, Stanley paced the Hall of Mirrors under a ceiling that spanned an awesome twelve metres in height. He felt hushed and reverential as he counted seventeen French windows on one side, matched by magnificent arcaded mirrors on the other. The room shone and reflected and chandeliers hung all the way down, like bunches of ice sculptures. La Galerie des Glaces, he decided, was the acme of sophistication. The woman who brought him here should be at his side.

> I would breathe down his neck
> had I any oxygen to expel.

Hearing other tourists enter, he turned around to discover that they had not. A warm prickle rose on his neck. He scratched it. He looked into a mirror. Was Versailles visited by the spirits his mother had seen? No sooner had he asked the questions than the answer came in the form of a woman standing behind him. Dressed in a nun's habit and wimple, she was no more than five feet in height and her tiny plump hands were folded over each other with a quiet confidence. When he swung around, she vanished. When he returned to the mirror, she was once more in view. Hers was a *métisse* face – not quite one thing, not quite the other, yet complete in itself. She watched him through clear, calm eyes, and her words tinkled like silver cutlery and delicate glassware at a banquet.

'There were no assemblies in the convent, except to hear the words of the Faith. No joy, except the singing of psalms. No warmth in winter. No decorative arts or fine foods. I did not choose a life of poverty and silence, monsieur. It was conferred on me at birth.'

Her voice did not come from her lips, which were as shapely and solidified as those on the marble busts around him.

'Whispered down these long corridors was my name: Louise-Marie, the Little Mooress, the Black Nun of Moret. It was at the Convent of Moret, with its cold stone walls, that I lived out the whole of my life. My mother, Queen Marie-Thérèse, visited when she stayed at Fontainebleau; otherwise I would never have known the art of conversation, such as she practised it.

'When the royal household moved to Versailles, she told me of the many festivals, the foreign emissaries, how music accompanied every moment of every day. Then I could think of nothing else. My own bedchamber, ladies-in-waiting, the prettiest gowns, all the young princes requesting my hand from the King.

'My mother told me that he was a countryman at heart who loved riding to hounds, he loved driving his horse at full gallop. He craved the forests, the hills, the rivers. Maybe one day, I prayed, the King will allow me a little cottage and garden.

'When my mother died in 1683, I cried without tears. There was no longer any hope. Her heart was encased in a silver box in the chapel at Val de Grâce, her coffin laid out in state. The Court went into official mourning. When my time came, I was buried in a simple plot behind the convent chapel.

'If only they had killed me at birth, because when I ascended the skies, there really was no St Peter waiting at the pearly gates, no everlasting happiness in paradise, as pure and virtuous as I had always been. Just this.'

Stanley's instinct was to pull this woman through the mirror, into the twentieth century. To dress her in slacks and a modest blouse, to initiate her into a world where she would have choices.

'Yes, just this,' he echoed, raising his arms as if to reach out. 'A half-life, neither here nor there –'

'What the flaming heck are you doing talking to yourself, Stanley Whateveritis Williams? Leave you alone for a few minutes and you've gone off your trolley.'

Jessie had replaced Louise-Marie in the mirror.

'I was talking to . . . the Black Nun of Moret . . .' Stanley trailed off, disappointed. He had wanted to empathize with the odd little creature. To say she made him realize how grateful he was to have had parents who made sure he was given opportunities that their own immigrant selves were not. How it was only when his father was old and weak that he began to feel compassion, albeit one drenched in resentment. She had prompted the question he now thought to ask Jessie: What was it like to grow up without parental love?

'You do have a sense of humour after all. Sorry for earlier, I'm an erratic bitch. Never said I was easy. Never said I was boring neither. Give us a hug, then.'

Jessie's cheek rested against his back.

'You're real, flesh and blood,' he said, as if he expected her to pass through him and end up hugging herself.

'No, sawdust and plastic. Are you done now? I've had enough of this poncey place. Thank God for the French Revolution. Let's drive to Paris tomorrow. I want to be among the living.'

No, he wasn't going mad, he reassured himself. A black nun. If he didn't tell Jessie now, it would be harder later. He began, tentatively, 'I *was* talking to someone. You won't believe this, but she's called Louise-Marie, an adult but built like a twelve-year-old . . . She's been wandering in this palace for over two hundred years, daughter of –'

Jessie flapped her arms. 'Was she wearing a white sheet and going "Oooooh!"?'

It really did sound ridiculous, but he persisted. 'She made me think of you. Raised in a convent without parents. What was it like, Jessie? Tell me?'

Battling a return of bad vapours that a café au lait and three iced buns had seen off, Jessie pressed an index finger to Stanley's lips. 'Joking about ghosts is one thing but turning it against me is another. I, Jessie O'Donnell, am lacking in nothing, so spare me your pity, Mr Nuclear-Family-Aren't-I-the-Lucky-One. Now let's get outside and get on that road.'

You must converse with her,
draw out the red ribbons of her heart.

Jessie steered Stanley out by the elbow. As they went through the door, he turned around just in time to see Louise-Marie's tiny feet, shod in dainty black booties, swooping over the floor towards him at a phenomenal speed.

Passing through him, she whispered, 'I try to imagine a man. Now it is too late. I can move through you and not feel you or me, monsieur.'

The Queen of France's Boudoir

Nabo, the Queen of France's black dwarf, tumbled naked off the four-poster bed, scooped up his doublet and hose, and rolled quickly underneath, just before King Louis XIV strode into the sumptuous boudoir for his twice-monthly conjugals.

Nabo watched as the thoroughbred legs of this accomplished hunter of the wolf, the stag and the wild boar climbed atop the mattress and disappeared from view, his frowsty black periwig plopping on to the floor.

Once again he had narrowly avoided the garrotte.

Lying beneath the royal couple, Nabo was aware that, unbeknownst to her husband, the Queen's thoughts were fixed on her *splendide*, *ravissant* and nabilicious *nain*, whose stunted height did not, surprisingly, extend to his bodaciously horny fifth limb. The Queen's famously puerile mind was the one secret apartment into which the King had no access, though should he ever be unlucky enough to find the key, he would discover that it really was devoid of furniture.

Life could be worse for the Queen's most cherished accessory. Usually the good life of a pretty Negro page, popular as presents throughout the Continent, perfect for showing off his mistress's fashionable pallor, lasted only until puberty. However, with Nabo's height and beguiling childlike looks, when he looked up at the Queen with big, dewy eyes, she was captivated. For ever and for ever. '*Pour toujours et toujours, mon joli petit garçon*,' she cooed.

What did he have to do for it?

Ram the Queen.

Queen Marie-Thérèse, born the Spanish Infanta, resembled the King as a sister does a brother; hardly surprising, as her father was the brother of the King's mother. Not much taller than Nabo, she would have been attractive, had her fondness for garlic and chocolate not made her teeth look like mushy peas and her forehead not bulged like a plumped-up cushion. Nabo's days were spent waiting on this capricious, voluptuous and indeed fatuous *reine* while she titivated herself in her bedchamber in preparation for the pomp of Court, where she was but an ornament to the royal pageant.

He carried her train with a studied formality. Fanned her assiduously in the summer. Held her smelling salts when her daily routine of inertia made her feel faint. Poured her tea. Fed her garrulous, beloved parrots. But alas, *alors*, the Queen became pregnant with child and, fearful of its negritude, was given to hysterical railings. When the child was born into the royal chamber, everyone gasped *Métisse!* The child was a *métisse*!

No amount of pleading on the part of the Queen made the King, who would one day inspire terror across the whole of Europe, stop spitting bile. When one of the doctors suggested that 'the colour of the child might have been caused by the black man's looking at the Queen', the King retorted, 'It must have been a very penetrating look!'

The little man vanished. He was extinguished from *l'histoire*.

. . . the royal infant that had just been born resembled a Negro dwarf that M. de Beaufort had brought with her from foreign lands – a little Negro that the Queen always had with her . . . When the Queen was better, I went every day to the Louvre to see her. She told me that everyone laughed at seeing the child, and the great pain their laughter caused her.

Mademoiselle de Montpensir, cousin of the King

There was no singing and dancing in the streets of France. No salvo of guns. No chanting of Te Deums. No bonfires. No fireworks. No church bells. No overflowing free wine.

Louise-Marie, the child was named, and she was hastily dispatched to the Convent of Moret, where she would be inducted into the closed sisterhood by the Mother Superior and her nuns, and remain for the term of her natural life.

A Caravan in a Country Lane

Neanderthal instincts and all that.
Stanley the Stud's bursting with lust,
his brain's gone on holiday and without it to hold the fort
his libido's completely unbridled.
Raw – we are both *sauvage*.

> I pull my trackies off, then hers.
> What happened to jeans and man's best friend – flies?
> I try to rip her knickers off but they're nylon.
> I stuff myself into her like banging a cork
> into a wine bottle with a hammer.

Got Stanley the Manly in my leg vice and I'll crack
his hips if I feel like it.
I'm grunting like a pig and pounding like a dog,
dig my nails deep into his buttocks.
You're not doing me, I'm doing *you*.

> Jessie the Ballbreaker, I don't think so.
> You want it so bad, you mouthy cow.
> I'm thinking Lucy Negro, I'm thinking Louise-Marie,
> I'm thinking Prince Charles & the 3 Degrees.
> Hip hip hoooray, I'macoming, I'macoming . . .

Need a soul of steel, me, tap-tap, anyone in?
Forged by a Sheffield blacksmith.
Instead it's Jessie what is Humpty-Dumpty.
Jessie what is Jonah, Jessie what missed the Ark.
Jessie what is napalmed.

> It's talk we gonna talk, Jessie.
> You're soaked through and the storm ain't done yet.
> You're clinging so tight I'm choking.
> What happened at Versailles? What happened way
> back when? Come on, Jessie, rain on me again.

You're a bad lot, a rotten stinking guttersnipe,
said that Evelyn Soames pinned to the ground,
red-faced and gagging. *You lot aren't invited*
to our houses for tea 'cos you're not respectable.
Everyone knows the orphans on the hill
'cause all the weekend trouble in town.

I was of no stock, let alone good stock
but good punching stock, aye, so take that on the nose
spotty flea-bag-seen-your-dirty-knickers Soames.

Like we weren't under lock and key after school.
Like we didn't fear the devil more than anyone.
Like we weren't good kids, real, real good kids.

Some things should be forgotten, sweetheart.
Some things take me back to first post.

You want my insides, Stanley, well, come on in . . .

The Convent

Sister Mary Patrick governed St Ann's
The Holy Terror or *Old Nick*
we called that Reverend Mother on account
of that switch dangling like a horse whip
from the corded belt of her black habit
next to the keys and brown rosary beads. We'd
do anything to avoid her in the puce-green
corridor, the tapping of her heels coming at you thirty
yards away on dark green tiles.
She was a demon risen from the dead – the sting
coming down on your naked backside.

You were born a sinner so whether
you'd been naughty or not punishment
was due and say thank you after.
You half-wit! You ninny hammer! You gombeen!

Now Sister Mary Peter ruled the nursery.
A flush-faced, beer-drinking puff of roly-poly ball
was the nearest I had to a mother, not

that she were allowed to touch her charges
beyond nappy changing and feeding. I'd
been dumped straight after birth. Me

and Mabel Calloway both shared a bunk bed,
were best friends but forced to hide it, intimacies
forbidden, convicts forced to sleep with arms

crossed over chests like *we* had the filthy minds.
What went on with those nuns?
Hoping we'd end up Brides of Christ like

all of them, sex-starved Sisters of St Ann's,
slotting between Old Nick and Roly-Poly Peter
on a sliding scale of evil and kindness.

Brides of Frankenstein we called them but not
all bad, like I say, just cold, most of them, like when
you're not getting it and deep-freeze sets in.

What did they expect when Curtis wrapped
me in his arms on Blackpool Pleasure Beach 1959?

It were so windy he said I'd fall into the icy sea
if he didn't shelter me in his too-tight tweed jacket,

handed down at St Andrew's Home for Boys.
They'd never had a lad so tall until him,

son of a black GI, six foot three and broad of back.
And why didn't we go down to where the boats

were moored, he said, find an empty one, never
had a cuddle before. He were only fifteen,

but I could smell his manhood. You see the nuns
hadn't offered sex education classes –

got sent to the coal hole for touching a boy
let alone kissing if someone reported.

After I'd done what I wasn't really sure
I was doing with Curtis,
we had a go on the Grand National Roller Coaster,
but it was still hurting between my legs
in between my laughter, roaring
Isn't this fun! Isn't this great!

Wasn't that I *felt* unloved like other whingers
who had two parents, a brother and a sister,
a home, hearthside fire, Sunday roast,
birthday cards and a pet rabbit.
I *was* unloved, proven fact, no parents,
just a house full of frustrated elderly virgins
what hadn't a clue how to love the seventy-odd
waifs and sad strays at their mercy.

Come from a long line of fallen women, me,
so had to uphold the family tradition, didn't I?

No one had to tell me my mother was
unmarried, underage, wayward bad,

but they did like to remind me I was born
into stigma and got my own stigmata

'cos Terry was so stubborn he had me
screaming thirty-two hours, a scar across

my stomach when he should have slid out
in sixty minutes I were that young and wide of hip.

And when I held him for the first time I cried
at how my own mother could've dumped me.

Couldn't leave my Terry for a minute, breastfed him
till he was four years old. You see no one

taught me mothering. I wanted him by
my side all the time. But he never listened to me, my

Terry was a disobedient teenager, tall
like his dad, wanting to go out playing

all the time like he didn't have family, like
he didn't have a home to go to, like

he didn't understand he was the first thing
that was all mine ever in my life.

Curtis was banished to a home in Birmingham,
me to a house for unwed mums in Nottingham.

My child up for a good Catholic home, they said.
Who me? My baby? Only thing I owned

wrenched out of my arms by blood-sucking bats?
I'd inherited something in my genes:

send a herd of elephants to stampede all over me
and I'll not be crushed. Maureen McCarthy

kindly took me in – St Ann's alumni,
cashier at Haycroft's Ironmongers,

in town while I looked after her kid and mine.
Once a month we went to the Mecca Ballroom

to hear Jimmy Saville spin the decks.
Then I discovered Ella Fitzgerald and started to mime.

Hate memories, me, they won't let you alone.
Didn't even own a pair of knickers till I was sixteen,

clothes doled out by laundry according to size.
Saturdays, when *normal* people, when *families*

went on picnics to the countryside, after
our breakfast of bread, porridge and cocoa,

the dirty laundry came out. I'd have to light
the fire underneath the old stone copper, being the

eldest, chuck in the clothes, pull them out,
run them through the mangle, starch them, hang

them up to dry in time for a dull dinner of spam
and hot vegetables from the kitchen garden,

mustard pickles and dried bananas for dessert,
left over from the war stockpiles, unluckily for us. If

you were naughty, you got condensed milk scraped
on bread all weekend. Saturday afternoons we

spent black-leading, polishing kitchen range,
white-stoning the hearth, mopping floors.

Tried aborting with the vacuum-cleaner hose,
preferable to a coat hanger, which was all the rage

in those days, but what was I thinking?
God forbid and thank God it didn't work, aye.

Once a month I was given two bob to go
to Mrs Fox's Toffee Shop at end of road,

buy a bag for everyone to share.
At Christmas, half a crown each to choose

from F. W. Woolworth & Co. Ltd in town –
courtesy of the Good Charitable Ladies of Leeds.

Now *that* was our heaven,
our paradise, our
Communion with God, our
short-lived happiness.

Café des Fantômes, Paris

Bronzed Art Deco floor circa – 1920s.
Indian-red armchairs circa – 1940s.

Frosted-glass counter on mahogany-panelled bar,
fresh yellow rose in a twisted clay vase,
starched waiter hovered, with a greased handlebar.

After a night rocking Jessie as her dutiful *amour*,
pouring childhood's misery into me, her one and only,
saying *au revoir* to her trusty welded armour,
she was softer, trusting, somewhat melancholy.

But I wasn't the one in need of stuffing up.
I didn't need no *petit déjeuner*.

O God! Crêpe flambé, steak in bilberry sauce,
waffles, pâté de foie gras, truffles,
I'm starving, Stanley, starving!

Simple breakfast will do: it's only 8 a.m., Jessie.

If you say so – her lovely, opened face, closing down.
She flipped the menu over. *Mein Führer.*

Deux croissants et deux cafés, s'il vous plaît,
I instructed in punctilious schoolboy French.

Posters in the alcoves were fake – Renoir.
70s cigarette vendor displayed – Gauloises.
60s juke box droned – Charles Aznavour.
Suddenly starring in our very own – *film noir.*

... See what happens when you let someone in –
get butchered in the heart and no doctor
can stitch you up; it's there for life,
opening and closing ...

Ex-husband Number 3, Mr Roderick Wilson

He was my matinée idol,
my Michael Caine as Harry Palmer.
Couldn't believe he'd wed me
from all those cleavages clamouring.

So I hung my pride up on the washing line
and watched it get soaked.

Told him I loved him several times a day,
so's he'd stay. Left notes under his pillow,
in his jacket pockets, his socks.

Said he couldn't breathe.
Told him to get an oxygen tent, didn't I

Said he needed time alone, to think.
Told him most people could think in the company of others.

(This one wasn't getting away.
I'd said for ever and meant it.)

Caught him sneaking out one night.
I need some space, Jessie.

That's when the carving knife
hurdled from its draw with the speed of an Olympic champion
and landed in my hand.
That's when he said he was divorcing me.

See what happens ...

My dear Jessie

I cannot
be a hod carrier
for someone else's soul

                    Love

             Stanley, dear

             tracing fingers
             through a window pane
             is not enough

                    Love

Because breakfast was not a banquet,
Jessie ate her croissant like a sulky child:

not bothering to brush flakes
from her nose, her chest, her mouth.

I wanted my rumbustious lover back,
to tell her that every woman I ever dated

demanded Stanley's Unabridged History
replayed/ verbatim/ once more/ with feeling,

or I'd be accused of withholding
(one pithy volume, remaindered, anyway).

You never talk, Stanley, about yourself.
Your father must be on your mind; it's not fair.
Last night I rinsed my lungs clean for you!

She scraped her chair back so noisily
its vibrations scratched over my teeth.

The waiter, frothing a cappuccino at the bar,
cocked his head, as if sensing trouble.

I'm going to the loo. Think it over.
Furthermore, I am NOT a gobskotch!

I wanted to shout after her, Jessie,
I'm not brave enough to excavate the dead,

to present my father on a cold mortuary slab
for a woman's psycho-sloppy autopsy.

Some things are better left unearthed.
Let him rest and let me rest, if you please.

Cette place est libre, said an intrusive voice
without the intonation of a question.

No, the seat wasn't bloody free, twat!
I glared up to see an incandescent creature

towering over me, a darker equivalent
of the Russian ballet dancer Nureyev,

possessed of the same hauteur
and barely bridled sexuality.

When I clocked the white bob-wig
drawn back from his forehead in waves,

showing off his rouged tawny skin,
creamy lace kerchief hanging in ruffles,

brocade waistcoat, the velvet blue breeches,
white silk stockings over athletic calves,

I guessed he'd sneaked in from the past
and hoped Jessie was suddenly constipated.

(For a drama was about to commence
in which I was merely an audience member.)

He slapped kid-leather gloves on to the table.
The waiter rushed over, rubbing his hands.

Le Chevalier de Saint-Georges
It is such an honour . . .

– Bring my rum concoction, lime, bitter, syrup
You will remember, two glasses, clean, this time
Fais vite! Je suis dévoré de soif!

On a mission of diplomatic importance,
the waiter brisked off, twisting his handlebar,

while another white-wigged man entered,
rubicund of face, this one was quite unimposing,

the warp and weft of his similar attire strained
by buttons all but popping off.

– Hector, you are late

– By the grand total of three minutes, Joseph

– You know I am a martinet about time
  Ah, I forgive your weaknesses, would that I had any

– To be perfect, Joseph. 'Tis such a burden, *n'est-ce pas?*

– Indeed it is. I have ordered my favourite rum punch
  It is sublime, my friend, sublime

> The waiter poured their drinks ceremoniously,
> napkin over arm, an ingratiating smile.
>
> Joseph sat opposite, languorously,
> as if the café were his personal fiefdom.
>
> Hector sat next to me, Michelin legs splayed,
> perched eagerly on the edge of his seat.

– *À votre santé!*

> They clinked glasses.

– This is a fine elixir with which you tempt me, Joseph

– And deadly, sweet as a woman, but take care
  when you go to stand up, you will keel over
  and decorate the floor with the hues of your colourful vomit
  Come morning, a sword is driven through your temple
  You have been warned

– Of the drink or of the ladies of this world?

– Both!

> Joseph chucked back his head, uproarious,
> clearly a man of great charisma and show.
>
> Hector dissolved into the first of three chins.
> He was clearly a man of titters.

– To the matter at hand. I sense my time is coming

– Nonsense! You are fitter than men half your age

– That may be, but my soul is weary

– Do not be maudlin, Joseph. 'Tis not allowed in my company

– I shall be myself because who else can I be?
   As I am a fine swordsman, so you are a fine wordsmith
   I invite you to write my biography
   My life has been accomplished, n'est pas?

– *Absolument!* And I humbly accept, of course
   I am proud to write about such an outstanding
   composer–swordsman–pianist–violinist–horseman–soldier
   –dancer–swimmer–skater and, if I may be so bold, lover

– Now, now, my head is swelling
   You know I detest flattery unless it is insincere
   Do I not have a reputation for humility and rectitude to
   preserve?

– Fear not: as your official biographer I will preserve it for you

– You must begin with my islands, Guadeloupe
   and the terrible Saint-Domingue where I grew up
   surrounded by waterfalls, thick pine forests
   the gommiers, the exquisite hummingbird
   and the volcano La Soufrière, which would rumble
   and emit smoke and frighten me as a child
   Above all, Hector, I grew up with sugar cane
   Sugar cane for Europe's sweet tooth
   She is such a monstrous evil bitch!

> He paused, tracing the rim of his glass,
> oblivious to Hector's obvious discomfort.

– The islands formed me, but *La Douce France*
   cultivated my talents

– So, must we begin with the islands?

– With my father, George, a Gentleman of the King's
   Bedchamber, and my darling mother, Nanon,
   a slave from Senegal

He bought her freedom. He never took mine away
At ten we sailed to Paris;
at twelve I won my first fencing match

– Such a man as your father is rare in these times, Joseph

– The privilege is given on a master's whim
You will remember my mother?

– We were all quite taken with her at our salons

– Not all. As for those who were affronted –
Who offends her, offends me, I threatened
Now listen carefully, Hector
The islands are a gaping wound in my heart
I fear I may never be allowed to return

– Why *did* you plunge yourself into the slaves' revolution?
Why become a malcontent when the world was at your feet?

    Joseph leaned forward in his seat so fiercely
    I jumped back in mine, stupidly.

– Slavery on Saint-Domingue is the cruellest anywhere
Plantation beasts are treated better
I fought, because I had to

    Hector pulled out a powerfully perfumed
    handkerchief and mopped his brow.

– Oh, let us drink some more of this poisonous bitch

– Millions have been enslaved to satisfy our lust for sugar

– Then let us partake of some wine, or should we overly
concern ourselves with the peasants whose feet
grow mouldy with the mashing of it?

    Hector trailed off when he noticed
    a flare of irritation sweep Joseph's face.

– My life has been truly serendipitous. I am of a rare breed
  for whom society opened their doors
  even as they despised my people

– Am I not your people too?

– Of course you are.

– Would that human nature was simple, Joseph

– *Oui, la nature humaine*

– My friend, you are one of the *people*, yet you supped with
  kings, sir
  With that charming dead queen of ours, Marie Antoinette

>   Hector ran a finger across his neck,
>   rolled his eyes –

– La guillotine. Urrrggghhhh!

– In spite of the fact that I dined with kings, sir
  Oh, when are you ever going to grow up, Hector!

– This is far too complicated for a simple chap like myself
  I will write about the *bon vivant* I know and love
  The man who skated over the lake at Versailles reciting Racine
  who was adjudged the best swordsman in Europe
  who at the age of twenty-one swam the Seine with one arm
  tied behind his back

  You were the first black colonel in the French Army
  You were prodigious: concertos, symphonies, string quartets
  How you once played your violin with a gem-encrusted whip
  How women swooned and succumbed . . .

– Nonsense! The gossip is greatly exaggerated
  I never had more than two hundred lovers
  I was most offended that my sobriquet was Don Juan
  Could I have been so prolific, if my mind was on my cock?
  Hector, be warned, you must not make me out salacious

– You will be portrayed as most sagacious, dear sir

– Nor must you omit how my invitation from Louis XVI
to direct the Opera was blocked by its leading singers
Our honour and the delicacy of conscience prevents
us from being subjected to orders from a mulatto
Gloss over neither the good nor the bad
but present the facts

– Surely such things were rare occurrences?

– I never dwelled on them
One day a fellow shouted *Moricaud!* on the Rue de Bac
I rubbed his face in the filthy gutter
There, now you are as black as I am. Noir comme les noirs!

    Joseph roared long and hard
    to Hector's spittle-filled giggles.

    Like percussive accompaniment,
    they made quite an orchestral spectacle.

– It will be a fine book, Joseph.

– Let us then toast the forthcoming bestseller
The Amazing Athletic & Artistic Accomplishments
of Joseph Boulogne, Le Chevalier de Saint-Georges
and His Astonishing Adventures in Many Posh Boudoirs

    Joseph raised his glass, but, before the drink
    touched either of their lips, he added,

– *And His Thoughts Emotions & Conclusions on the Terrible*
Evils of the Trade in Slaves & the Inhuman Conditions
under which They Suffer, as Perpetrated in the French Dominions
as Witnessed by Himself

    Then his eyes swung over to mine
    and I felt the power of a great seducer

capable of spinning others into the vortex
of his own pain or passion.

– And you, my friend from another age
have been privy to my private conversation
Sadly, Hector died of gout a few weeks after our meeting

When Napoleon sailed the Great Mother Ship
called France, I fell prey to national amnesia

I beg of you, make of me a memory once more
Let me be known

They froze, glasses raised.
The waiter passed through them,

clearing the cutlery away, clanking
down a saucer with the bill.

L'addition, he sniffed, standing there
like a policeman while I sleepily

re-emerged into the twentieth century
and rummaged for my credit card.

my people came out of nowhere, Joseph, were transplanted
on to on an island, and memory began with Clasford's folks,
Ida and Wilbur, straight-backed, Presbyterian cane-cutters,
living out an obscure death in a dour studio portrait

and Evangeline Avery, Pearline's mother, crippled
by cutlass-wielding husband George,
who ended up face down in the creek for five days,
because he wasn't worth fishing out

my people come from a straggly, disgruntled queue
of slaves, masters and indentured servants,
of whom I was never allowed to speak –
the hoe, the road, the rape, the tongue split by a knife,
then slowly ripped apart like the tough, succulent
flesh of the yucca

shame, shame, shame *Doan go raking up the past, Stanley*

Pearline, born within two decades of the nineteenth century:
she could reach out of her basket,
touch its cusp with the twentieth, stroke the weals marking
her great-grandmother's elephant-hide back

long before she and Clasford moved to London, and taught me
to honour my parents but not those who went before,
stuffed anonymously into an airless attic trunk
with moth-eaten clothes and discarded mementoes

shame, shame, shame

Clasford always said that Jamaica delivered him and England
destroyed him, but he was wrong, Joseph, you see
both formed him – one with the sun, the other with rain

as you were the bastard son of the islands and La France
and you dared to make that difference your own,
so I will discover my difference and make it my own

The Camargue

Take a risk, come with me –

To where the chests of valleys have collapsed with their final
prehistoric breath

Miles of wispy conifer plantations, spines bending with the wind
in a parade of arbour-aerobics

Freshly burnt clumps of bulrushes heaped alongside the sinewy
tongues of canals

Soft-flowing meadows where hay has yet to be scythed
down into spiked and angry stubble

Flamingos gather on mud flats, rubbery necks flopped over as
their bills search for food in the shallows

Corps de ballet
Scarlet skies
The Camargue at dawn

Savannahs of rice paddies, as if Vietnam; salt-pans and pyramids,
as if Egypt

Bulls' heads nailed to the doors of the herdsmen's thatched
cabanes – a tribal motif

Choreography of wild white horses charging across marsh and pasture

Listen –

To the hypnotic chug of the car's engine, like a damaged third lung

To the pursed whistle of oxygen coming in fast through the open
windows

*Dear All. Driving through a postcard. Glad I'm here and not there.
Showing off. See you – whenever (ha ha). Stan x*

Morning in a French Lay-by

'Do you believe in an afterlife?' I asked Jessie one morning, bringing her a cup of tea in bed. I love the morning-Jessie best, soft and cuddly, before she dons her chain-mail for a fresh round of jousting.

She yawned, voluptuously creamy legs sprawled on top of the pretty yellow and white flowery duvet. I wanted to rearrange it, to make it more artistically messy, with her supine form sprawled across it.

'What a thing to bring up first thing in the morning,' she chided, her voice throaty with sleep and the residue of sex.

'It's important. I want to know,' I insisted, before I bottled out.

She cleared her throat, gaining remarkable speed, volume and voracity within seconds.

'Put it this way, it was drummed into me at St Ann's that if I didn't go into the confessional box every Saturday from the wicked old age of twelve, and uttereth in my most penitent voice, "Bless me, Father, for I have sinned. My last confession was a week ago and since then I've committed mass murder, masturbated myself blind, masterminded a bank robbery and burned an effigy of Christ in a voodoo ritual in Roundhay Park at midnight" – well, then I'd burn in hell. 'Course, I wasn't quite the reprobate you see before you today and I was in hell anyway, so what's the difference. Soon as I left that place I decided to take life by the balls and give it a good twist. Far as I'm concerned there's too much focusing on the hereafter and a lot of suffering on earth as a consequence.'

It wasn't quite the answer I'd hoped for, nor the speech. I sorely wished that I'd mastered the art of manipulating a conversation. That I knew how to keep one going instead of prematurely closing it.

'At least they instilled moral values. People do need a spiritual life, to believe we're being looked after by a benevolent, omniscient force.'

'Not disputing that: it's the heaven and hell scenario what I hate. Any chance of a jam sarnie to go with this cuppa?'

'What about spirits? Do you believe we come back after we've died?'

There, I'd said it. Or had I?

'Hope so. I'm coming back as an elephant and all those who've wronged me will come back as centipedes. Gotcha!'

'Ghosts!' I blurted out. 'Have you ever seen one?'

Jessie emitted a vulgar, scoffing laugh, prolonging its initial impulse until it rang hollow and fake. It was then that I had a little revelation: she didn't really know me; nor I, her.

'I'll tell you what happens. Six feet under, and worms. That's as spooky as it gets.'

She yawned again, this time with arms outstretched, revealing horrendously bushy armpits, which I'd never noticed before.

She began to slide off the bed. 'C'mon, laddie, let's get to Spain before lunchtime.'

Got my own ghouls, Stanley, dear –
the nameless mother who shamelessly left me,
the named father who could have rescued me,
the son who selfishly deserted me –

getting in my way when I'm walking,
popping in my head when I'm talking,
creeping around me, stalking.

A Thousand Miles from Home

It was so blue-rinse, so retired-couple-touring-the-shires, so, shall we say, cheap-holiday-home-on-a-site-in-Essex, and, when overtaken by those ubiquitous jet-propelled palaces on wheels towed by Mercedes-Benzes, it felt like dragging a pathetic farm truck packed with cows. Once we hit the southern sun, it was different. Suddenly the caravan felt lightweight, bouncing along behind us, smoothly able to handle Jessie's screeching brake stops and deadly swift mountainous turns.

We circumnavigated the big cities, looping back or threading through to pick up the coastal roads. Barcelona. Tarragona. Castellón. Valencia. Alicante. Almeria. Malaga. We climbed the curlicues of mountains. I was awed by the sheer drop to olive groves so far down they looked like rows of bonsai trees. We'd find a deserted valley and camp for a few days: the joyous absence of man or machines, the whole of a morning sky; sounds only of the natural world – rivers, birds, and, well, things like that.

When I came, I heard myself rebound off mountain walls because I hollered for the first time ever, because for the first time ever no one could hear.

We continued on our journey, the sea view disappearing behind high-rise apartments or flat-faced pueblos, ridged terracotta roofs clustered on both sides of the road.

The surprise of rounding a bend and seeing the sea spread before us, like silvery turquoise foil.

I became adept at packing the camping accoutrements in the caravan: everything was secured in cupboards and suitcases so that nothing fell out en route. Jessie was cook and driver. I assumed the role of co-pilot and house-boy, and, no matter how many times I complained, I had to tidy up after her all the time. I knew that if I kept on at her, she'd change her dishevelled ways.

I learned how to wash with a beaker of water and a lemon, which

I thought a bit extreme, actually, but Jessie said it was part of my survival training. (What's she like.)

She was impressed at the speed with which I calculated the sterling–peseta equation. I convinced her to get a road map, and I learned how to follow foreign road signs quickly, and how to stay calm when she shouted at my mistakes.

'All you've got to do is navigate, Stanley! I'm doing the hard work.'

'Why don't you let me drive, then?'

'Would you really want *me* as your co-pilot?'

I stopped protesting.

The car became our protective bubble, intimate and intense, just the two of us, simultaneously inside and outside.

And whatever secrets lay between us, when submerged, ceased to exist.

The Campsite

Hippie types, retired people, procrastinating students, debt-dodgers, and us. Like I said to him, the site was perfect and we'd nabbed the best view of the sea before the tourists descended like a plague for the summer.

It was a large site on a hill and we were tucked away at the bottom so there'd be no campers gawping at what we were eating and whispering their verdict, thinking we didn't know they'd got nothing better to talk about.

Stanley said the sea looked like frothing blue beer. I took the hint and sent him up to the bar to get some.

So there we were, sitting by the sea. 'Spain smells differently from England,' he said with the kind of profound gravitas reserved for someone who's just discovered the theory of relativity. 'The heat, roasting chickens, campfires, grass, fresh fish in town.'

''Course it does,' I said, pointing my finger northerly. 'Countries that don't smell are the ones to avoid. Clinical equals bland equals bloody fascist.'

'You mustn't generalize,' he said, adopting his banker-speak. 'No one nation is homogeneous, no matter what its PR machine says. Did you know there were black people in sixteenth-century England and eighteenth-century France, *par exemple*? Who knows what's in the genes of your average Frenchman or Briton today?'

I really didn't know how his mind worked. Where did that come from?

'Oh, homegenoff, you big show-off.' Then I massaged his limp little self, and he said I always knew how to shut him up, in the nicest possible way.

We slowed down to a full stop.

Months of hedonism do that to you.

Summer on the Coast

Like a dusty, ramshackle field for refugees, the campsite slowly became littered with households turned inside out: self-styled kitchens with open-plan dining rooms cum through-lounges, hammocks slung between trees, portable showers hidden behind plastic sheeting, washing lines with dripping towels, swimwear and underwear standing in for the boundaries of garden gates. Cars, mobile homes, caravans, combi-campers, motorbikes, bicycles and tents were pitched higgledy-piggledy with no regard for town planning. The gentle murmur of spring was drowned out by the rush and drone of summer season traffic on the road below, which separated the campsite from the sea.

J Couldn't have asked for a more gentle man than Stanley. Gives me no trouble at all. Summer was the best ever

S Well, we wake up at first light, spend all day on the beach, sleep when the sun goes down

J Still opens doors for me, walks on the *gentleman*'s side of the road

S To elaborate: I fall into this sun-drunken stupor during the day. At night, I barely recover

J Got our favourite spot at the far end of the lovely sandy beach away from the hordes, a stripy-blue umbrella, a flask, sandwiches

S I enviously watch wind surfers with their sea-butterfly wings, but I won't waste money on something I might not be very good at

J Attention-seekers, I call them

Citroëns with sagging suspensions hauled Morocco's extended families down from northern Europe as they headed towards the ferry at Algeciras, roof racks piled up with refrigerators, televisions, sound systems, all strapped on with rope.

The beaches were caked with flaked-out bodies, gunged up with cream and sweat, forming a second, shimmering, undulating skin.

S So here I be, Stanley Orville Cleve Williams, doing his *thang* on a never-ending holiday with a gorgeous woman, who can't get enough of me

J I bought him the Complete Works of Dickens for his birthday. Now his head's always stuck in it

S She snatches my book and runs off into the sea with it, again

J Come and get it, lover-man. Whooo-oooo!

S Her dimpled cheeks shimmer so sexily, I'm mesmerized (still)

J Better hurry up or Nicholas Nickleby will end up drowning, or can he swim?

S Whoever invented the thong should receive the Nobel Prize for Services to Mankind

J What about Oliver Twist? I reckon that wretched little mite needs a good bath. Or did they have jacuzzis in the workhouse?

S I chase after her to retrieve it, jumping up and down like a madman while she dangles it out of my reach

J Back at our spot, he tickles me as revenge. I'm begging him to stop, tears streaming

S I want ice cream! she screams until I give in out of sheer embarrassment and go get some. When I return, *David Copperfield* is buried face down in the sand

Gangs of leather-clad riders wrapped in black sunglasses and seated on low-slung motorbikes cruised along the coast with unhelmeted recklessness, as if the trip from Germany had taken but an hour and they were really winged raiders in a sci-fi movie.

Package-tour coaches converged, clogging up the coast's arteries, offloading pasty-faced hopefuls outside the forecourts of sprawling resorts and ferrying them back with blistered noses and infrared shoulders from Marbella and Fuengirola to the airport, thereon back to the North's insipid sun and inevitable drizzle.

J When I wake up, he's here. When I turn around, he's here. When I go to sleep, he's here. Can't believe my good fortune

S Minutes give birth to hours, hours to days, days to weeks, weeks to months

J Too hot for the beach now — we sit under the awning of the caravan with bags of ice on our heads

S Let's drive to the upland village of Mijas tomorrow, I suggest, licking up iced water as it tumbles over my lips

J To be honest, I thought we'd already done the grand tour of Spain

S I'm desperate for a change of scenery

J Are you saying my ugly mug's not good enough any more?

S It's just that I'm going stir-crazy. Hey, it's not personal, Jessie-Baby

J We can't have that, can we?

S We passed a field of sunflowers facing the sun that resembled rows of beatific Stepford-like devotees being communally married at a cult rally

J It's torturous driving in the heat without air conditioning. Do I complain to Stan the Man? No

S Stout old women in mourning black, chalky-white houses with green shutters, a string of red peppers dangling from a wall – the real Spain

J Yes, the real Spain, where they sell *chocolate con churros*, thick drinking chocolate dipped with doughnut fingers

Senegalese men with the lope of gazelles hawked goods up and down the coast, arms draped with baubles, and sarongs, which were really headscarfs back in Dakar, and bead necklaces, which were once pods on West African trees.

Gaudy amusement arcades whirred, clunked and squawked next to empty afternoon discos that, undeterred, blared the latest Euro-techno-beat.

Britain, France, Ireland, Belgium, Germany, Sweden, Denmark and Holland catered for their nationals with restaurants, pubs and supermarkets, conceding only to Spain's fresh bread and vegetables.

'Catering for those who want to turn abroad into home,' Jessie commented, as they sat outside a café under a striped umbrella. 'They want the sun, but they can't stand foreign, except when the natives dress up in colourful costumes and dance for them. How sad is that? Now us, we're *independent travellers*.'

S I keep expecting another ghost to appear. I miss them

J Has these conversations – in his head. I can see his lips twitching

S If only Mum were alive, I'd take her on holiday to the sun and the sea. It's what she left behind

J He won't give me a penny for them

S We'd visit the most ostentatious palaces and have fun detecting passing ghosts

J So long as he's by my side, I shan't ask for more. When he's ready . . .

S I vaguely remember . . . I was such a small child . . . seeing a queue of cars at traffic lights turn into horse-drawn carriages

J Stanley calls me the Calor Gas Queen. Tonight I cooked paella, steam rising off it like a miniature volcano, with salad

S I'm good at salads

J Yes, the way he washes lettuce is nothing short of miraculous

§ I've bought a guide book, much to Jessie's disgust, as they're for tourists, not *independent travellers*

J For dessert we had aniseed cakes, macaroons, pastries bathed in honey. Then he goes and spoils it by saying he wants to go to Ronda tomorrow. Another dead village

§ A dappled-grey donkey meandered up some steps, like a tired farmhand returning from work, lost in his thoughts

J Hills, streets, squares, a river gorge, an old bridge . . .

§ Jessie, we've got to go see the Palace of the Alhambra at Granada; otherwise it's like visiting London without a trip down The Mall

J We don't need villages or any more oversized houses like that Versailles. Don't need anything but each other, do we, Stanley?

§ I've started to long for a walk alone, along the beach at sunset, to collect my thoughts before they go completely awol

J Space? Look at the sky overhead. Look at the sea yonder. Look at the mountains behind us. There's space, if you want space

§ There's not one of me any more. I'm a proper twosome

J We're a knuckle and joint; separate and we'll dislocate

§ Gibraltar is only down the road; I'll be gone a few hours

J We'll go together. When the season's over and the weather's cooler

§ You're right. Gibraltar is for the lowest form of humanity – tourists. Let's leave it. And anyway, I just lurve vegetating

J It's called relaxation, Stanley. I'm saving you from a future pace-maker

§ Oh, look, surprise, surprise, the sky is blue today, again

J You can't let your puppy dog off the lead; before you know it, he'll be humping some young bitch in the bushes

§ I listen to the radio wittering on all day long: Jessie FM

J If it's one thing I'm good at, it's communication

S She clings to me while sleeping; there's a sticky film of sweat between us, but if I try to budge, she grips tighter

J You have to savour it while it's here; save up some loving memories for later

S There's a reason why the City Fathers created the two-week holiday. All this free time. I need to be *doing* something

J Are you saying you want to go home to your nine-to-five?

S I wouldn't want to be anywhere else or with anyone else (God, I sound like Clark Gable). Now take this tissue and wipe your eyes

J So, we'll relax while it's hot, set to some money-making ventures when it's not

S And stop using my plastic fantastic? I'm not used to spending more than I earn

J Do I detect a mean streak in you, Mr Williams? Our rent here is twenty pounds a week!

S The mechanics of my brain need WD-40. My dick too. It's all going to pot

J Less than once a week now, which I put down to the heat. And I'm the one who always has to initiate, which is boring

S When you get it on demand, it becomes less desirable

J When he goes to the pump to fetch water, I worry he's never coming back

S I should have been a marine biologist. So near the sea, its pull becomes irresistible

J He sits for hours staring into the horizon. Let me in, for a change

S Did you know that only 1 per cent of the ocean floor has been explored? I'm longing to disappear in a deep-sea submersible

J Lovely, I reply, a nice little cabin for us with a king-sized bed, a bottle of Moët et Chandon and an audience of perverted, voyeuristic fish

S What's for bloody dinner!

The Crying Mountain

It was the end of summer, the campsite all but deserted. That evening the sea had been like bark, and the air glutinous with the humidity that precedes a storm. The sky was portentous with thundercloud and the guttural squalls of seagulls. Inside the caravan, Jessie and Stanley had made a frantic, sticky love, more impelled by the desire to relieve the pressure drumming inside their heads than by a carnal, craven passion.

It had been raining for days, the worst rainfall in twenty-five years along the coast; the roads were waterlogged and hazardous. When the mother of all storms finally exploded, the River Fuengirola burst its banks, erupting out of the mountainside in a thunderous explosion, sending vehicles head over heels, flattening houses, uprooting trees, claiming several lives and (as the final obstacle in its flight path) sweeping up the campsite and carrying it forth to sea in its terrible, unstoppable arms.

The thundercrack awoke Jessie and Stanley, and immediately afterwards the caravan was lifted up in the full blast of breakneck rapids and hurled over the road, where it ended up smashed into a tree. Where the sink had been, the gnarled tentacles of branches reached in to grab the occupants. They held on tightly to each other, barely conscious and barely breathing, as the river and rain washed over them, pounding the windows on each side of the bed. But, thankfully, the caravan did not collapse them.

They prayed to a god both had abandoned long ago that they would not be carried away.

The Civil Protection Service arrived shortly thereafter and they were driven to hospital to be treated for bruises and shock, before being taken to emergency accommodation at Hotel Enriqueta in Marbella.

The next day they were able to survey the damage. Matilda, they were told, had been drifting out to sea until the tide decided to bring her back. Although the car was now looking decidedly forlorn and muddy on the beach, it was remarkably undamaged. But the garage mechanic told them it would suffer from salt erosion in the future.

The caravan, he confirmed, was a write-off.

Seeing Red in Orange Square, Marbella

S

J

old town, narrow streets
boutiques, Arab wall
how I *long* to be a tourist

my little caravan
now it's gone, my
summer second to none

rain
missionary of the skies
cleansed

trauma's supposed to bond
like cement, not sink
like subsidence

flood – emissary of doom
aftermath, we face
off

Villa Express Letting Agency
'A lovely flat
overlooking harbour'

I can see clearly
rpt, rpt, rpt
now the rain has . . .

only £60 a week
he can afford it
(bank statements)

my nest egg
will not be siphoned off
by my credit card

S   J

Mr Sugar Daddy
becomes Mr Skin Flint
(you never know people)

and another thing –
when will I see the colour
of your silver?

was always my intention
to supplement
my savings = safety net

£400 fucking squid
you're taking the mickey
Jessie

so let's get enterprising
make money, move
easterly

oh, sure
summer = bumming
winter = freeloading

who, just *who*
plucked you
from your sodding hellhole?

manna offered
manacles clamped
manumission sought

I give 100%
nowt to be ashamed
blameless

S

two interlocking circles =
ideal = 50% =
more than enough

sleep in Matilda
until we get sorted
tired, Stanley, *so tired*

viciousness
never knew existed
it's . . . exhilarating

hearts
already got shards
sticking out

face screwed up
like she's mental
God, I'm evil

where's my
sweet Stanley
gone?

c'mon, retaliate
usual Amazonian spirit
spear in one hand, tit in other

scooping
my eyeballs out
but he's gone so cold

S

old Governor's House
arched balconies, shields
everyone's staring

two choices –
cuddle in arms?
follow yellow brick road?

she's shouting
but my legs
just-keep-on-moving

J

he's wearing jeans
not trackies
traitor

he's striding off
come back, Stanley
come back!

Rock of Jabal al-Tariq

Sunset had transformed the Strait of Gibraltar into streaks of flowing magenta and fuchsia scarves.

Feeling the last rays of sun penetrate his cream woollen pullover, Stanley peered through a telescope at Morocco's Atlas Mountains, which lay as misty peaks within his imaginary grasp some ten miles away.

He had arrived in Gibraltar a day earlier, fascinated by the novelty of this limestone rock that adjoined Spain but that was one of Britain's last remaining colonies. He soon discovered that aside from the sight of red double-decker buses and red phone boxes transplanted on to a distinctly Spanish-looking town, there was little else to interest him.

Morocco did fascinate, however, and he had spent the afternoon hovering around the port, deciding whether to take the ferry over to Tangier the next day. It was a trip lasting all of two hours, but one that would place him for the first time in Africa – the continent where some of his family tree had begun one, two, maybe four centuries ago. It would be a momentous decision, yet he was afraid that if Europe was opening little skylights, through which he could see that its history was more than he'd ever realized, then surely Africa would open whacking great doors, through which he might never return. He knew little of Africa beyond the popular image of starving peasants and corrupt governments, and it seemed too vast a territory to contemplate navigating until he was ready. It was for package holidays to Egypt or Kenya, or for real independent travellers, not for kidders like himself. Aware that he was talking himself out a major adventure, Stanley recognized his old self peering cowardly above the parapet, the self who weighed up the cons and dismissed the pros. He decided that Africa would be for another time. A properly planned trip.

Moreover, leaving Europe would sever the potential for any contact with Jessie, perhaps for ever.

After their altercation in Marbella, unable to breathe properly or think clearly, he had taken off along the coast, bought a rucksack and given away those vile tracksuits to a hotel cleaner. He began to pick up some Spanish. *¿Hay un hostal aqui cerca? ¿No tiene algo más barato? ¿Cóm éste in español?* He would research a town and its history, select somewhere cheap to sleep and enjoy the company of strangers. A simple interaction in a bar, maybe a bullfight on the television, a crowd of men gathered to watch, and he, one of them, sampling herbed olives, sliced sausages, toasted almonds, beer.

It was a pleasure to know that his soap would still be in the exact same position where he had left it last; that his watch lay unharmed by the bedside cabinet and had not been clumsily knocked down behind it; that he would no longer have to wade through women's clothes when he went to the bathroom in the middle of the night; that each perfect squeeze of toothpaste was his and his alone. He realized how much he had missed talking to people, how Jessie had dominated conversations to the point where he became the mute, compliant partner, registering pity in the eyes of people who would look kindly upon him, as if he were a bit slow.

But with the hindsight that comes with passing time, Stanley's triumphant departure began to seem foolhardy, no matter how hard he tried to deny it. She was never far from his mind. He began to dream of those silky breasts that spilled out of her negligee and pushed up against him in the morning, nudging him awake. *Did you just offer me a cup of tea, love?*

When he bought another hunk of bread and another chunk of cheese from another mini-market in another strange city, he salivated over her effortlessly and deliciously stir-fried peppers, onions, mushrooms and strips of beef, sprinkled with soy sauce and served on a plate of moist noodles.

When he brushed his teeth at night and looked in another bleak mirror, in another bleak bathroom, in another bleak hostel in another bleak part of another strange city, he saw congealed shaving foam on his jawline – stuck there all day because she wasn't around to affectionately wipe it off with a wet finger.

And the silence, which he had so welcomed at first, was getting noisier every day.

Jessie, Jessie, Jessie. Wherefore art thou, Jessie?

He traipsed to Cordoba, where he discovered that the Moors had ruled Spain for eight hundred years. In Cordoba alone there had been hundreds of shops, street lights, libraries, air conditioning, central heating, hot and cold water piped into houses and sophisticated advances in medicine and science. It made him want to storm up to his history teacher, grab him by the lapels and demand, 'Why didn't you tell me about the Moors, Mr Cartwright? Why not, eh, why not?'

As he explored the past, he became aware that the past was exploring him too, in its own spooky way. Life on earth was just the beginning, he now understood. He craved another visitation. Like an addict, he needed his fix.

In Granada he went to visit the Alhambra – *Al Qal'a al-Hamra*. He wandered around its reconstructed palaces, its lavish landscaped gardens, its courtyards, its lily ponds.

He saw it floodlit at night.

He wanted to reach up

snap off an iced turret

feel a little bit of history melt in his mouth.

Stanley strolled over to a bench facing the sea and closed his eyes. The sea wind tickled his eyelashes and brushed his lips. He licked the salt from them, liking the taste. It was a wind that had swept all the way up from Africa, gathering energy and ferocity, passing through swamp and jungle, mountain and valley, over desert and savannah, until it finally arrived at the beaches of Morocco and tore across the strait.

When someone began to speak into his right ear, though there was no sensation of a body beside him, Stanley grinned.

About time, he thought. About time.

The voice was sibilant wind.

'It was here that Jabal al-Tariq crossed over to his namesake, Gibraltar, in 711. At Janda Lagoon he went into battle with his army of fourteen thousand men against King Roderick of the Visigoths, who had a greater army of sixty thousand. Jabal al-Tariq turned to his soldiers and said, "Whither can you flee? Behind you lies the sea and before you the foe."'

There was a pause.

'Did they defeat the Visigoths? They had no choice but to. Thus began the conquest of Spain. Before you lies the sea, Mr Stanley, which you are not yet ready to cross. Behind you is the woman you left behind. Whither can you flee? Whither can *you* flee?'

'I must find her,' Stanley said determinedly, surprising himself. Whether he spoke aloud or to himself, he wasn't at all sure.

'Because you cannot run away so easily from the person you are running away with. You must stick together to complete your mission.'

'That's very grand. My mission is what, exactly? Damned if I know any more.'

'Of course you do. It is to get as far as you can go by land because this is the way to discover that your footprints are tracking ancient, well-trodden ground. Allow me to present myself.'

Stanley opened his eyes to see a very thin, sable-coloured man sitting upright next to him. Wearing a saffron-yellow turban, he had a small white goatee and matching yellow robes. His cheeks were drawn, his skin porous and without sheen; deep wrinkles fanned out in waves from the ridge of his magnificently hooked nose. Stanley saw that his eyes had the distant, almost mystic look of ancient tribes captured in the early days of photography.

'Zaryab – named after the precious bird with dark plumage that is possessed of the sweetest voice. Banished from Mesopotamia by my music master Isaak when my talent outgrew his. After a long journey I arrived in Cordoba in 821 with a thousand songs stored away that I was required to sing from memory for Caliph Abdur-Rahman II. Was I a happy man? I had lost my wife. I had lost my children. I had lost my country. I was in exile. A thousand tears were stored in my heart that I released into song. It is terrible to lose what is dearest to you, for ever. Of this I need not tell you. Do not be responsible for leaving this woman so callously. You will regret it the whole of your life and, I must warn you, for the infinity of your death.

'As to my fate, in time I settled into al-Andalus and accepted my losses. How did I keep myself busy? I introduced the first conservatory of music. I created the fifth string for the lute. I introduced the flavoursome cuisine of Baghdad to this region. I set the fashion for changing dress according to the four seasons of the year and I introduced toothpaste and quilted gowns for mountain nights. I helped make everyday life a little more beautiful, a little more practical, a little more sophisticated, a little more luxurious, a little more learned. This is how great civilizations are created, by little men like myself.'

What have you invented, Mr Stanley?

Unsure as to whether he was asking the question of himself, or being asked it by his visitor, he realized that the man's voice was somehow indistinguishable from his own thoughts. It was a most disorienting experience.

'Don't make me laugh!' he blurted out defensively. 'Mr Stanley fits into the system, or he did until recently. A cog in a wheel, etc. I'm not the guy to invent a *new* wheel.'

'Then you can become such a man. Our motto was "Know Thyself". We were true seekers of knowledge and therefore seekers of Our Creator. My time was an era of conquering, building and consolidating. The complacency that precedes the downfall of all great civilizations was still many centuries away. As yours is but a century away.'

There was another pause. He studied Zaryab's dignified face, like that of an exiled king who still feels responsible yet is helpless to protect his beleaguered kingdom.

'When Granada finally fell to the Christians in 1492, the same year Mr Columbus sailed to another old world, I witnessed our capitulation and I was devastated. Everything we had built up – ah! Soon after, the Moors were expelled from Spain by Queen Isabella, and the light went out for centuries.'

Zaryab began to sing, his voice falsetto and rich in coloratura:

Weep for the splendour of Cordoba, for disaster has overtaken her,
Fortune made her a creditor and demanded payment of the debt.
She was at the height of her beauty; life was gracious and sweet,
Until all was overthrown and today no two people are happy in her streets.
Then bid her goodbye and let her go in peace, since depart she must . . .

Opening his eyes, Stanley saw that night had draped itself completely over this part of the world. A part of the world where the fingers of one continent reached out so tantalizingly towards the tips of another.

What was he supposed to do with these time-travelled tales?

A full moon laid out a path on to the sea.

Zaryab appeared, walking in front of him, the most regal of ghosts. His yellow dress caught and shimmered in the moonlight. He stepped out on to the sea, treading its silvery road. His voice floated back with the wind: 'I often come here, to remember the time when Africa began at the Pyrenees.'

The moon tipped backwards and slid down to the other side of the world.

The sea had become a cauldron of smoking black oil.

The Room in Jessie's Head

Oh, for Crissakes, Jessie, what have you gone and done this time?

What the hell do I know! One minute Stanley and me are in it together. Catastrophe hits. The next, he's gone off in a major huff. Had I caused the flood? Was I responsible for Belsen? Did I drop the bomb on Hiroshima? A pettifoggin' argument – over what?

Was it really over filthy moola, you know, money?

Not all of it. You know what? I'll tell you why: it's 'cos like that Evelyn Soames said, I'm a rotten stinking guttersnipe and no one sticks around me for long. When I'm in crisis, the devil suddenly snaps off the *Linda Lovelace Porn Special* on XTC TV and zooms drunkenly into my orbit on his pitchfork, waving a bottle of gin in one hand, and giving me the finger with the other. And where's God when I need him? Sitting in front of JC TV with a glass of home-made (reduced sugar) lemonade and watching *another* rerun of *Little House on the Prairie*.

Did you fall, Jessie? Come on, be honest now.

You fall in, you fall out.

Not good enough. Try again.

If you don't label it, you can retract it when you've been dumped. Don't give me *that* look. Oh, all right, I was swollen with feeling for him, like when we held each other at night. Was like sleeping with Terry before he outgrew Mum's bed. He was such a good, dear boy. I was beginning to think he'd last the course.

How did you feel after the bust-up?

Put it this way – I felt every man who ever loved and left me had started swinging at my insides. George Foreman's fists were in there and Muhammad Ali's, and that Henry Cooper's too. And no, it wasn't the Rumble in the Congolese Jungle but the Rumble in Jessie O'Donnell's Tummy. Oh, forget it. Look, I thought I'd left that all behind. I thought Stanley and I were travelling into *our* future. But all of a sudden he's back-pedalled and I'm struggling uphill on one of those children's scooters what Santa Claus never left for me when I was a kid.

Yeah, as the saying goes, 'Life's a bitch and then you die.' In the meantime, what did you do?

First night I kept vigil by the window. Second night I kept hearing his key turn in the lock and I'd be bursting with joy and forgiveness for like five seconds. Third night I cried myself awake. Fourth night I cried myself to sleep. Fifth night I knew he wasn't coming back. Sixth night I either had to pull myself together or dip into my savings.

So what are your future plans, Miss O'Donnell?

Should I go home? To what? Put it this way:

Nuns left a pile of shillings for the gas meter
on the ledge by the front door –
as if we'd dare.

Used to wonder if those coins'd take me
on the train to freedom
in Manchester or London.

Never stopped dreaming of escape,
but where to? Who to?

To this day can't see a train
or a bus without wanting to hop on it.
Got to keep moving, me.

How are you going to do it, Jessie? Stay on the road and survive?

Working on it. What is my USP? What do I have to sell?

Yeah, because as the song goes, 'Pick yourself up, dust yourself off . . .'

It's not any old song any more. It's my flaming mantra.

When and where were you happiest?

Obviously with Terry and Kwame. And nine days ago the rain stopped awhile, the sun came out, and Stanley and I woke up from a siesta to a rainbow wearing a stripy polo-neck sweater, arching its spine backwards over the sea. I linked his arm and we stood there outside our caravan. A perfect moment, which I thought we were sharing.

Stanley or Terry – if you had to choose?

Don't be daft! You don't know love until you've carried a child inside and devoted yourself to its upbringing. Still, Stanley was such a special lad.

Go on, admit it – do you miss him?

So very, very much.

Not dropped that madcap idea of driving to Australia, then?

It's not madcap, smart arse. Yes, it is. No, it isn't. Yes-no-yes-no-yes-no. Oh, shut up. Look, it's what keeps me going. I want my son back . . .

How would you like to be remembered?

Oh, go to hell!

Mama Hortense's Singing Kitchen

'I'm a cook, contralto and comedienne. Any offers?'

That's how I met Sergio and Eeva-Lina. He was Spanish, from the interior. She was a Finn who went on holiday, fell for him and stayed. Ingratiated myself by becoming their one regular for a week. A right funny pair, seeing as she was topping six foot and he was nearer the five foot mark. She was a strapping long-legged ex-model with scraggy bottle-blonde hair and two-inch black roots, who wore foundation as subtle as hardened cement. Her teeth were a state. Heavy smokers. Both were. Eeva-Lina carried herself like a Viking goddess (what doesn't know she's gone to pot) and had that desperate expression of fading beauties craving admiration in the gaze of others. Sergio had the kind of moustache that'd put you off kissing a man 'cos you'd be wondering what hatchlings lurked inside it.

I'd exhausted myself trudging around the fringes of Marbella, seeking out little bars and restaurants in need of a good shake-up, and came across these two, desperate for business – my last shot. I appeared to them as a fairy godmother (my speciality) when I said I'd cook up a storm and turn their run-down café into a culinary establishment and cabaret bar. Eeva-Lina had named the place El Smorgasbord, in spite of any evidence that she'd ever sliced a salami, let alone sold one. A marketing gimmick, she explained, over-enunciating as if English were *my* second tongue, and ruffling her hair, carelessly blowing smoke in my face like she was Greta Garbo returned from the ball and I was Hattie McDaniel waiting patiently to take her fur stole. It's clearly worked, hasn't it, I refrained from saying, casting my eyes at the empty chairs. Instead I pitched forth, 'Mama Hortense's Singing Kitchen, right? Let's start afresh.'

They looked affronted, which made me push my cards further up the table. 'Give me licence to make changes. Are we agreed?' They shifted uncomfortably and sneaked the kind of coded glances at each other that a blind five-year-old could decipher. I collected my bag and jacket and got up to leave. 'Or I'll find somewhere else.'

That forced them to nod. Sergio's was two beats behind Eeva-Lina's, as he'd had three bottles of beer since I'd arrived an hour earlier and was breaking open the fourth with his teeth. 'We'll specialize in Caribbean cuisine,' I stated. (Who's to know any different around here.) That made them twitch excitedly, and Eeva-Lina suddenly clicked pretend castanets in the air and shouted, 'Carmen Miranda! Josephine Baker and her swinging bananas. Olé!'

I let it pass.

'I'll rustle up a kaftan, make a bandanna, big silver loop earrings, bangles, ruby lips and guess what? Big Mama's in the house!'

Sergio smiled, revealing his muddy pearlies. I wished he wouldn't.

I added, 'After the overheads, we'll split it forty–sixty.'

It was a statement. I was still standing and turning slowly towards the door, so they didn't argue.

The new signboard went up. The kitchen was clean enough but tiny. The eating area was 'compact' and 'rustic': grimy, grey concrete walls, cobwebbed wooden beams, a bar decorated with pebbles and shells stuck in these dollops of plaster, ashtrays made from upturned half-coconuts. I got them to wash it all down and paint the walls sunny yellow while I went off to shop for stock.

I cadged some old concert posters from a tourist agency and put them up, stuck a few candles into old wine bottles. I rehearsed some songs and psyched myself up for showtime. It had been years.

Thursday was opening night. Sergio's drinking cronies were in, thinking it was freebies all the way, which he encouraged, playing some kind of second-rate Don Corleone, while they devoured my chicken curry. I was dressed up in a 'tropicana' kaftan – a print of parrots surrounded by lime-green and metallic-blue flowers – but I wasn't going to get on stage for those louts, so I put Ella Fitzgerald on instead. Sergio left with his crowd well after midnight and didn't show until an hour before opening the next evening, grinning idiotically, sauntering drunkenly in the door, while Eeva-Lina hurled several wine glasses at him that smashed into the street outside. Then she darted into the kitchen, emerged with a knife and rushed at him, cursing, *Senkin saatanan kusipää! Mä vihaan sua! Saat nähdä, sä toivot vielä ettet olisi ikinä syntynytkään!*

I restrained one business partner and sent the other off to sober up.

Sergio's bank manager was in on Friday. 'Course he didn't pay either and I wasn't doing a show for one. Against Equity rules, I told them, when the audience is the same as or fewer than the cast.

Saturday – we got twelve Irish tourists who'd prebooked, only to walk right out again when they sniffed the whacky-backy Eeva-Lina was blowing out her nostrils. She was lounging by the bar in a PVC cat suit, red, seventies, and so skin-tight it rode up her crotch.

I told her to put it out, to which she replied, 'But tis is Marpella.'

Sunday – two passing couples were seated and actually eating when Eeva-Lina took it upon herself to jump on stage (I just knew she'd been itching to get up and show off) and start to do these ridiculous catwalk poses (white leather hot pants, white boots, white cellulite), singing out of tune 'Vallink in love akain/ Vhat am I to do/ Vhat am I to do/ I cahn't hilp it.'

It was hysterical. The audience thought so too. They didn't leave a tip.

I noticed white powder on her nose.

Each night Sergio walked off with the takings in a canvas bum-bag. Wouldn't let me check.

The next day I hawked myself around the hotels and casinos, but, as I thought, no one was interested in a clapped-out-has-been like me. Humiliating? Yeah, ain't that the truth.

Least I got three meals a day at Mama's. My only outgoing was rent. But I had to issue an ultimatum or it was skid row for Jessie. First – no drugs consumed on the premises. Second – no drunkenness. Third – no freeloaders. Last – no impromptu performances from ex-models.

Mama's Rule was established, which made the Lazy Losers sulk and bang about for a few days. I let them. I was too busy cooking and doing a thirty-minute set each night. I'd remember customers' names, make them feel special, so's they'd return to show off their cabaret star 'friend' to their pals. Things picked up through word of mouth.

Truth is, I was powfagged. Up at 9 a.m. and in bed at 2 a.m. Truth is, I was working with a pair of Lazy Losers. Truth is, I just couldn't get over how Stanley had gone off so suddenly. Where was my baby boy? Truth is, how was I ever going to get to Australia?

Closing Time at Mama's

'I'm gonna wash that man right out of my hair!'

It was how I ended every evening, singa-longa-mama, guaranteed to get the audience going, especially if a group of women were in, like a hen night, demanding yet another encore. Surprising, really, seeing as they're supposed to be celebrating a marriage. Sweat ran down my forehead from the bandanna and poured from every crevice beneath my kaftan. I wanted to scream *Gimme yer flaming gelt and bugger off back to your three-star hotel, you lot!* when this vision appears in the doorway, with the kind of sheepish grin usually associated with criminals who've been caught in the act of thieving and hope their charm will get them off. A person I'd not seen hide nor hair of for so long I'd forgotten how very *masculine* he was. I wanted to jump off the stage, or rather the wooden crates passing for one, and bite into his juicy little bottom.

I finished the song, got my tips, saw the customers off, then ambled over to the bar for a rum and Coke. It was the same sort of stroll I'd last seen him engineering in Orange Square.

I didn't know how to play it or whether to play it or what. My heart was thumping so hard it was hurting. My mouth had dehydrated, so I downed the rum and Coke in one and was about to pour another with uncontrollably shaking hands when I was held from behind. I went so weak-kneed that I began to sink to the ground, but he was holding me with those long, strong arms that I thought I'd never feel again, and he was apologizing for the manner of his leaving and he was . . . brimming.

Now, I'm not one to show my tears – we have a special relationship based on privacy. It's a pact we made, oh, about forty years ago. In any case, they prefer the moist warmth of my ducts and will do anything to stay inside. What the heck, I admit it, I betrayed their trust.

Out of my peripheral I caught my 'business partners' skunking off into the kitchen, snickering at the show Mama Ballbreaker was making of herself.

Said he'd missed me rotten.

'How can I trust you not to throw another wobbly and leave me in the lurch again?' was what I wanted to say but couldn't, what with his pitiful, tearful eyes.

Once we'd both blown our noses and acclimatized, I smirked. 'I'll give you a lesson you'll never forget. Bend over.'

'You what?'

'Bloody bend over.'

I looked at the kitchen door. The Losers were still in there, injecting, ingesting, snorting, licking or whatever it was they did. Stanley bent over and I gave him a good spanking. Thirty smacks, really hard. We fell into fits of convulsion, the way you do after you've been crying and opened up. Felt him get hard. Horny little git.

'What are you doing here?' he asked, finally straightening up, wiping his cheeks with the backs of his hands. 'I heard about Mama Hortense and I just knew it had to be you.'

'Running the New York Marathon in a Donald Duck suit. What does it look like, Stanley? I'm trying to survive.'

He hung his head at that, and so he should have. I explained the circumstances of my current situation and he swung into action. 'Okay, show me your business plan and I'll see if this enterprise is feasible.'

'What planet are you on?'

'All right, then. Show me your books.'

'Do you think I've had any time to read books? I don't even get eight hours sleep,' I said mischievously.

Look, I told him, it goes like this. Sergio pockets the takings, deducts the running costs, claims he divvies up the profits forty–sixty.

Stanley thought for a minute, then said with delayed and, I've got to say, sanctimonious outrage, 'You can't stay here with those leeches. Let me cover costs until we make some money. Is that agreeable to you, my lovely Jessie?'

'You are such a good boy!' I squashed his cheeks in between my hands, turning his lips into the kiss-up pout of a fish. 'Let's move on to Greece: it's cheaper there. We need to keep going – Australia's a long way away.'

'Yes to the former.' He paused, chewing his bottom lip like he didn't want to ruin our new season of goodwill. 'You're not really serious about Australia?'

'Look at any map of the world. Land mass all the way to India, at which point we put Matilda on to ships. Simple, if you've got faith.'

'Jessie O'Donnell, you are well and truly nuts.'

'That's why you came back, you great barmpot.'

The Alps

'Snowy, cold, empty, icy and bloody dangerous. In other words, they're to be avoided in winter unless you're the kind of person who likes jumping up and down with two planks strapped to your feet or, more sanely, to be cosily ensconced with your (nearly) toy boy on a rug in a chalet by an open log fire sipping Armagnac and looking out of the window on to their distant snow-capped, mountainous pomposity.'

In spite of Jessie's protestations, we were climbing the Alps. After crossing the border at Menton, we had driven off the autostrada, leaving the coastal roads behind as we headed inland to satisfy my curiosity.

We slept in hostels, and one night we slept in Matilda, parked just outside Monaco, where accommodation was too expensive. Earlier, the *gendarmerie* of that Great Kingdom of Casinos had ejected us as 'illegally sleeping aliens'.

After several weeks of tentative reacquaintance – *Excuse me, but do you mind if I put my penis in now? Are you sure? Oh, that's lovely. Here it comes* – we were back on form and had shot up the coast to France and headed towards Italy. Thereafter we would go to Greece and thereafter?

I was learning to live in the present.

Yet I had also accepted that I was driving into a future I could not plan and into a past I could not control.

Jessie's profile leaped out with such vitality as she drove against a backdrop of blustery southern European landscapes. I was able to stand back and study her these days, while I listened to the constant retelling of her stories of past woes and dramas. I sympathized, which was what she wanted. Yet she now seemed to fear my natural quietness, agitated if I was silent for too long. I realized that her endless chatter was supposed to keep me close, like a rein.

She still didn't want me out of her sight. At first I didn't mind. God, did I listen:

All those hours, months, years,
amplified tick-tock of the clock
in my bedroom-cum-lounge-cum-kitchen,
while Terry was at school learning the independence
he'd use against me, eventually.

Jangling nerve ends waiting for the jarring
brrring! brrring! vibrating from the pay phone.
Ewan from the Coach and Horses:
Fifteen pounds. Cash in hand. 8 p.m. sharp.
Yea or nay? Plenty'll be grateful if you're not, Jessie.

Postman opening the garden gate
and me, running down three flights of stairs to check
and never an invitation to go to London
and discuss your future plans, Miss O'Donnell,
not one lifeline out of hell.

She took her eyes off the road and nodded expectantly, as if to
indicate *Your turn.*

And say what? Instead, I delicately suggested she let go of past
sufferings. Whereupon she shot me the kind of blatantly distrustful
look that accused me of being a very *recent* perpetrator of crimes
against Jessie O'Donnell.

I guessed she was right.

We swept through deserted valleys with mountains in the fore-
ground or in the shadowy, surreal distance, suspended mid-air with
clouds rising above and beneath them.

Crevice. Cornice. Crevasse. Precipice. Gullies. Spires.

Helicopters deposited dynamite to precipitate avalanches. Trees
wore white hats. Prehistoric paragliding birds with single wings
flew overhead. Cross-country skiers wore primary-coloured ski-
suits, blue, red, yellow shaped *z*'s of padded nylon zigzagging a trail
of shaved snow, disappearing into forests or seemingly over the edge.

We wound upwards towards isolated terraced hamlets, and down
towards the tranquillity of a deserted lake surrounded by a prayerful
assembly of fir trees.

I could smell pine.

It was revitalizing.

High above, springs burst out of the hillside like frozen stalactites.

'You mentioned Terry earlier.'

We were looking into the green lake, the blurred forms of trees reflected in it like swaying nuns.

An underground stream rumbled beneath our feet.

'Tell me more about your son?'

It was a question I had asked when we first met, and she had stormed off into the bathroom, returning with puffy eyes. This time she shook her head mysteriously. 'When you love someone, you must let them go. If they're meant for you, they will return. Like you did, Stanley.' As if reconsidering, she added, 'If not, you might just risk seeking them out.'

When she started back up the track, she suddenly looked so forlorn. A hunched figure submerged in a navy-blue duffel coat, hood up, hands in pockets, dragging her trainers in slush. I wanted to run after her to ask what had gone wrong with Terry. As if sensing my intent, she spun around, threw off her hood, vigorously shook out her Medusa plaits and, squinting in the surprisingly fierce sun, called out, 'If not, make effigy of said person and go to the witch doctor.'

What a crazy woman she was.

'Now let's get out of here, Stanley. Mountains are a reminder of how insignificant we are in the order of things.'

'There's something so spiritual about them,' I declared enthusiastically as I joined her on the track, feeling I had to defend them. 'They were here before we came and they'll be here after we've gone.'

'You're very sweet, but don't be fooled: we're nothing to these imposing fascist bastards. Let's move on, otherwise we'll be in the papers next spring when some unfortunate anti-social shepherd whistling a folk tune, wearing thick socks and knickerbockers, knapsack slung over his shoulder stuffed with hard bread, mouldy cheese and cheap red wine, comes across a defrosting, decomposing black hand sticking out of the snow.'

'Don't be so morbid,' I said, chortling, as we got into the car. 'Let's go further up.'

I'd acquired new leverage since my return. So.

We set off for the top, Jessie muttering almost inaudibly under her breath.

Somewhere in the distance, another avalanche was being exploded.

Dusk began to settle around us surprisingly quickly.

The setting sun turned white peaks aflame with crimson.

The ascent was exhilarating: the whole world dropped away at our feet as we headed into the new unknown.

Then I began to see movement, here and there. Indiscernible objects that almost took shape before they disappeared, then reappeared as, surely not, elephants! Laden with packages? When I peered more closely, they became translucent and faded away. Suddenly huge rocks were being thrown in front of us. Or were they people hurtling to their deaths? An alpine wind sounded like a falling man's reverberating cry. Behind us, the march of heavy feet. Or was it the engine's rumble as we staggered up ever steeper inclines? Down in a ravine, fires were burning like little candles in the growing darkness.

I cast a sideways glance at Jessie. She was concentrating on the increasingly precipitous winding road.

Rounding a bend, I saw a band of soldiers: short men, African men, burdened with baggage, carrying shields, swords, javelins strung across their backs. They were weary. They wore crude leather boots and the ragged pelts of skinned animals. They were gone.

Inside my head was a voice that bristled with a gruff, no-nonsense machismo.

Never seen snow or mountains,
scorching white or burning cold.

Never seen the scale of them,
how man's bones could fill with ice,

then, frozen numb, snap off
like brittle branches, one by one.

I was born Hannibal of Carthage,
son of Hamilcar 'The Lightning' Barca,

250 years before your Jesus Christ.
And it was my life's duty to honour

my dad's intent to take the army of Rome,
who patrolled the Mediterranean

with their flash ships and falsetto sailors
as if they owned the very sun itself,

the sun that turned *my* Carthaginian Sea
into sheets of glinting, hammered brass.

But the Alps were not the desert
or the forests steaming with humidity

and teeming with wildlife that me
and my soldiers knew so well.

To cross it with an army was to come up
against a ruthless triumvirate:

Emperor's Mountain, Snow and Ice
And their ever-faithful ally General Cold.

Need I tell you, Mr Second-in-Command,
no one had effing done it before.

We were in danger, I was now aware. The road was not much wider than the car and slippery with black ice as it wound itself like a snake around the mountains. The higher we climbed, the colder it became. At each bend I hoped we'd reached the peak or come to a wider platform so we could turn around. The snake was controlling us. It was squeezing the life from us.

Jessie was quiet. Very, very quiet.

Finally, she spoke: as slow as the wheels of the car. 'Need chains on the tyres ... Road needs grit ... Some daylight would help.'

I could say nothing.

'Can't mess with these monsters. All this for the sake of adventure? Not *my* idea of one.'

We drove on in silence. Damn! This was my fault. This was how tragic deaths occurred. Firstly, you find yourself in danger. Secondly, you find yourself dead.

'Where's God when you need him?' I whispered, worried that the weight of my voice could adversely affect the mechanics of the car.

'Where do you think?' She replied as if it was obvious: 'Watching *The Waltons*.'

I closed my eyes and prayed. When I opened them, Jessie was sighing with relief. We had reached the summit. She cheered, cautiously. We began our descent.

Suddenly I heard a clunk-scraanch. I let out a pathetic yawp. Something was packing up. The brakes? The flood? The rust? We had been warned.

Death was chasing us.

Jessie automatically began some strange braking manoeuvre with the hand-brake and clutch, which scraped noisily as she jerked the car forward. She was tightly coiled over the wheel, every facial muscle exuding a phenomenal will power. She was grinding her jaw. If I poked her, she would detonate.

There was no one behind us. No one in front of us. We had not seen another car for hours. Matilda's headlights were our eyes, because we were in the pitch black that no city really experiences.

'Have you made your last will and testament?' she joked, without a trace of humour.

What could I say to that?

'Well, who else are you going to leave it to?'

I put my hand on the door handle.

'You're not going to leave me, are you?' She sounded disconcertingly neutral, as if she was trying to hide a terrible fear or a terrible rage. 'Isn't this the point in the film where we say we love each other?'

No, this is the point in the film where we die, I wanted to reply.

'You wanted adventure,' she added bitterly. 'As for jumping ship, you'll not last the night out there.'

My voice broke through: 'I wasn't going to leave – how could you even think it! *I'm* the man; I should have taken responsibility for the car.'

'Are you really?' she sneered. 'Remember, *you* left me when we should have been sorting out the car, Stanley Stone-Age.'

For all her front, I heard tears swelling inside her words. I looked over: she was blinking them back.

She was right. *Mea culpa*, Jessie. *Mea culpa*.

I realized then that she hadn't forgiven me for leaving her.

Where was this Hannibal? Why couldn't these ghosts make themselves useful for once?

80,000 infantry, 12,000 cavalry
and forty fucking war elephants, armoured.

All decked out with banners and bells,
turrets holding archers and slingers,

trampling enemy tribes underfoot
who fled my trumpeting mammoths,

followed by my swordsmen, who ran in after
for the blood-squirting slaughter.

But it was no joke, mate, no joke
to face battalions of ice up ahead,

to stand on the tottering edge of a ledge
in snow storms and avalanches,

watch thousands of my men fall below,
with no bushes or rocks to hold on to,

just smooth ice and dissolving snow.
To see terrible despair in the face

of every hardened soldier remaining
– except yours truly.

Ice was replacing the marrow in my bones. How could I face death? I was just beginning to live. It wasn't fair.

We weren't quite starting, nor quite taking off. Jessie was inching us forward. Any minute we could be freewheeling. Over and out.

I had no goodbyes to say. My friends would miss me, but, well, yeah, they'd get over it. My parents had said their farewells. Jessie and I would go together.

Soldiers were up ahead. They had reached an impasse. The road was blocked by rocks, upon which logs were burning. To keep them warm? Standing apart from the soldiers was a dusky, bearded man, with tightly curled hair that sprang out like unruly corkscrews; he was built like a boulder himself, his features deeply ingrained. Minions ran back and forth relaying his orders. This was a man not to be messed with. This was, of course, this Hannibal.

When he looked at me, history ceased to exist. We were in the same place. We were in the same time. And I was calling for help.

Once the fire raged strong enough,
we poured vinegar over the rocks,

which helped them crumble
so my men could set to hacking them

with iron tools, and opened the road
for our three days of descent

to a lower plain and woodland,
to valleys, grazing ground and rivers,

where we made fires, set up camp
in a place more fitting for human habitation.

We never took Rome, but we harassed
those arrogant shitheads for 15 years.

Listen, if we could cross these mountains
with a tropical army and trumpeting elephants,

surely you can do it with one dodgy motor
(and one dodgy missus), mate.

'We're going to be okay,' I reassured Jessie, who tutted and didn't respond.

Sure enough, we were: a moment later we rounded a bend and the road began to flatten out until it was horizontal again. Somehow we had managed to arrive at the bottom of the mountain, because somehow time had ceased to exist.

'What we needed was that mighty atom Hannibal,' Jessie said, once we'd turned right on to a main road.

Hannibal? What did *she* know about him?

'Crossed the Alps with an army and elephants. Lost upwards of thirty thousand men in these mountains, he was that hell bent on getting to Rome. Didn't make it, but he gave them a run for their money for fifteen years. In the end, the Romans attacked Carthage, which Hannibal had to go to protect. Killed himself, rather than be captured.

'He's my one and only true hero, Stanley. Why? Because he kept his crew together in the face of adversity. Because he was a wily little git with big brains. Because he had courage and determination to reach his goals, even though these mountains threw every obstacle they could in his path.'

'How on earth do you know about Hannibal?' I asked, shaking my head.

'*Everyone* knows about Hannibal.'

We were driving carefully through two mountains that rose as dark walls on each side of us.

Ahead in the distance were the muted lights of a town.

'Now another pugnacious little midget, that Napoleon, crossed the Alps nearly two thousand years later by an easier route and much better pathways. He said Hannibal was the most audacious military genius of all time, who at twenty-six years of age achieved the impossible. That's Hannibal, who drove on, regardless.'

'Hannibal, who drove on regardless.'

'No, Australia.'

'Australia?' I echoed weakly, a croak in my voice.

'Yes, Australia, Stanley, Australia.'

The Fêted House of Medici, Florence

Saliva dribbled down his chin in globules, where it hung wobbling precariously from the tiny, dread-locked balls of his beard. He swayed around the streets of Florence in greasy, blackened rags, hair matted into two clumps that stuck up like obscene horns, into which twigs were embedded. He was separated from the other pedestrians by a force field of the foulest stench of human decay and waste, emissions that had first seeped from his openings and pores a long time ago, the addition of fresher secretions helping to maintain a layer of artificial skin.

Alessandro, the infamous tramp of Florence, was a familiar sight to the local populace, who paid him little attention. It was only when he raved at customers sitting outside restaurants, spittle landing like squirming tadpoles in a bowl of seafood soup or on top of a char-grilled steak, that he was chased by irate waiters cursing, *Levati dai coglioni!*

J Breakfast-time at Trattoria Augusto and the lukewarm sun sinks its nutritious rays into me after that horrendous journey via the Alps

S The sun enhances the honey-dew texture of her skin. Jessie is simply glowing

J Stanley's at my side and Terry's still in my sights, so – fingers crossed

S The mountains are behind me forming a physical and, yes, a mental barrier between me and my home. I passed their test and they released me. I wonder if I can ever turn back

J Hope he feels guilty for putting me through it. Not apologized, yet

S A cobble-stoned piazza, bars, restaurants, crumbling façades, a fountain of sandy marble, Poseidon ruling over it with his three-pronged fork, pigeons paying homage. It's a charming Italian square until convoys of tourists emerge to destroy the view

J Have to agree with you: Italian cities improve with age, whereas English ones just look miserable. Here they're so beautiful and –

S Atmospherically picturesque and wonderfully evocative as seen in vintage Fellini?

J Took the words right out of my mouth, dearie

S You'll come and see the sights with me, then?

J Look, you go and be a typical tourist and I'll just be typical. Better still, you explore the Renaissance and I'll explore the restaurants

S And so, in this amazing city renowned for its Renaissance culture, with galleries, chapels and museums aplenty; in this city whose history is inextricably intertwined with that of the Medici banking family; in such a city, my lover prefers to sit in a restaurant and savour the tastes of the cuisine, prompting me to ask the question: Will she ever change?

J Put it this way, my boy here wanted his freedom and me, slave master, giving it him

S An old woman in black scatters bread crumbs among the pigeons from a brown-paper bag, clucking and cooing as if they were her children. Cyclists cross the piazza, carefully avoiding mothers pushing buggies. A middle-aged man in a biscuit-coloured jacket takes his morning espresso, leaning on the counter of a bar. He looks like a smart businessman but gets into the driver's seat of a taxi. A party of Japanese tourists is shepherded along and, even though it's 1989, people turn to stare, just as they do at Jessie and me, casually but noticeably. If it's with hostility, I've learned to ignore it

J You can thank me for that

S I do! I do! I do!

J Keep your hair on, we're not at the altar yet. Now, where's that waiter with our breakfast? Starving, me

S She leans forward and uses her arms to lever up her breasts, which pop up from her low-cut T-shirt like two veined rugby balls. The waiter's eyes nearly fall out, which I suspect is her intention

J He's got to see I'm desired by others

S It's that croissant-spitting time again. My beloved's eating habits have long since ceased to be endearing

J Sometimes when I'm eating, he looks so irritated, like I shouldn't be enjoying myself. Not my fault he's not a foodie

S I look at the sky; so does she. I rub my nose; she does too. We've reached the stage in our relationship where we subconsciously mirror each other. I thought I'd broken it, but (I cough, a moment later, she coughs) we're still . . . merging

J When you're done with seeing how the dead are venerated, whether they were picturegenic or not, when you're done with glorification of the Catholic Church, come back to Mama for some lunch

S And now, my beloved, I'm off to be a tourist, a soul tourist

J Sloping off with that lean, loping gait of his in those *jeans*. Looks like a schoolboy whose legs have grown too quickly. Bit too jaunty for my liking. Got to let him go, though, haven't I (should've offered to look after his passport)

S I turn around to wave. She seems a bit distraught, then switches on a fluorescent beam. Zzzing! I smile back, to reassure

Knapsack over his shoulder, arms swinging side by side, Stanley walked down pavements so narrow he almost fell off into the path of a speeding Vespa rider. As he made his way up Borgo degli Albizi, he quietly whistled to himself, looking forward to seeing the dome of the Duomo in all its tressellated glory.

187

Alessandro was lurking on a street corner. He picked out Stanley, thinking, I'll wipe that smile off his backside, *happy bastardo*.

As Stanley turned right into Via de' Castellani, an obnoxious smell hit him. A flooded sewer? Garbage? When he felt a tap on his shoulder, he realized it was human. Turning around, he was faced with the execrable Alessandro, so he began to run, with Alessandro in flapping pursuit. '*Per favore.* You must help me!' Embarrassed by the stares he was receiving, Stanley bounded up a pedestrian side street lined with the imposing studded doors and grilled windows of large houses, and darted into a dark alley flanked by high walls on each side – and at the end.

Cornered, he shouted, ready to defend himself: 'What do you want?' Alessandro was about to lunge at his prey but clearly had second thoughts and sunk to the ground, blocking the entranceway.

Stanley groaned and sank too. A moment ago he had a morning of historical sites in front of him; now he was imprisoned in a dead-end by a bundle of rags. At his feet were empty cigarette packets, wine bottles, a syringe and an apple so crawling with maggots it looked like a tiny brain. He kicked it away.

'It's not fair,' Alessandro moaned.

'What's not bloody fair?' Stanley shot back.

'Guilio de' Medici, my father, was Pope Clement VII, but he did not want to know me until I was thirteen years old and he only brought poor *piccolo* Alessandro to Firenze to be his pawn.' He began to whimper, not bothering to wipe his nose.

'Stop snivelling and get on with it,' Stanley growled. This thing was obviously no threat to him whatsoever. What an idiot he was for running away. Superwimp Stanley, you *know* what you are.

Alessandro began to talk again, rapidly. 'Giulio made me live in Florence with Ippolito, his great-nephew, but we despised each other. When Giulio first proclaimed me Duke of Florence, he protested, "Why should it be him! That muulaatooo bastardooo!"'

Alessandro rocked himself back and forth.

'I was the sole ruler of Florence and I could do what I liked. So I did. How else did I come into this world if *mio padre* did not do what he liked with *mio madre*, Simonetta, a slave girl from Africa?

What about your Henry VIII, who was my peer, or all those other rulers who were so perfectly awful? O no! Blame *me* for everything. What if I did kill Ippolito? Was he nice to me? No! Did he insult me? Yes! O! Life was too horrible until my kinsman Lorenzaccio came to Florence. He became my friend, my saviour, my handsome lover. We dressed up in women's clothes and charged through the city on a horse, knocking down those stupid people who got in our way. It was his idea. It *was*! Then the Council accused me of dishonouring women. "Women have no honour," I explained to those imbeciles. "So I give them the benefit of mine!" They should be *grateful*. All those stupid Fiorentinos complained because I trained my canons on the town. You tell me this – should I let them rise up a *second* time against me? O, but my story has such a sad ending. My Lorenzaccio was secretly very jealous of my great power, so he and an assassin stabbed me to death while I lay in bed waiting to enjoy a girl. I was a mere boy of twenty-six. *Fine di Alessandro.* How *terrible*.'

He flung himself on the dirty cobblestones, pounding them with his fists; then, stopping as abruptly as he had started, sat upright and said calmly, 'They were all wicked to me. No?'

Stanley's rear end had become stiff on the chilly ground. He wanted to escape the claustrophobia of this madman's death and despair, to venture back into daylight. Alessandro made him think of his father: although a good man, he too was bitter, self-pitying, accusatory. Clasford never rose above being a victim, one who had been betrayed by the life he had chosen to lead. 'Once a foreigner, always a *blasted* foreigner' had been his motto – tattooed on to his psyche.

Was he, Stanley, really an outsider? Maybe you didn't have to blend in or be accepted to belong. You belonged because you made the decision to and if you truly believed it no one could knock it out of you. These visitations came from inside the body of history, turning its skin inside out and writing a new history upon it with a bone shaved down to a quill dripped in the ink of blood. Europe was not as it seemed, Stanley decided, and for him, at least, Europe would never be the same again.

'Sounds like you deserved it,' he said coldly to the snivelling Alessandro.

'You are too cruel! You must restore the reputation of poor *piccolo* Alessandro so that I can sleep. I have not slept for . . . one . . . two . . . three . . . four . . . so many centuries.' Crouching, he craned his neck up to the sky with an expression of childlike bliss. 'O! To sleep, for ever.' Frozen in this position, he then swung his eyes back to Stanley with a demonic glint. 'It is my right. I am Medici.'

'The city was a better place without you.' Stanley was enjoying being self-righteous. His self-worth had just been raised a notch. 'If you are dripping in your own shit in perpetuity, it must be your punishment. No?'

He stood up and strode straight through Alessandro, relieved to be bathed once more in the sunlight of the street outside. At least he was a decent man, a free man, a living man. Whatever bad things you do on earth will haunt you when you are dead. *Evil com bak like boomerang*, his mother used to say. Well, he'd never willingly hurt anyone, had he? Jessie couldn't have been too devastated by his departure in Spain; otherwise she wouldn't have welcomed him back so quickly. In fact, wasn't he the one who was more upset by the whole scenario? And what did that Zaryab say? *Know thyself.* Well, he'd spent his entire life thinking there was something wrong with him and there wasn't. He was all right, and he was getting better.

'*Arrivederci*, Alessandro de' Medici. *Arrivederci*, arsehole.' He turned around, expecting to see a pathetic figure in chiaroscuro, a figure lifted from a religious oil painting: tragic, haunted, supplicatory. But the Alessandro who stood in the alleyway was removed from his dingy surroundings by a theatrical spotlight of sunshine that had broken through the narrow panel overhead between the high walls. He looked like the dashing lead actor in Shakespeare's missing thirty-ninth play, *The House of Medici*.

Stanley's spine crawled with ants.

Alessandro's face would have been striking but for the dissolute glimmer in his eyes, which were damp with self-pity. The puffed sleeves of his red and purple doublet were sewn with luminous diamonds, rubies, pearls. He wore a gold codpiece and black knee-breeches over thin legs. From his boyish shoulders hung a lustrous silvery-green gown trimmed with fur.

He looked extraordinary. He looked overblown. He glistened and bedazzled and the sweetly sick scent of vanilla poured out of him.

Alessandro whispered, 'I had a daughter, Giulia, and a son, Giulio – a lovely golden boy of four years. He was my life. I lost him.'

He shook his head. 'He lost his father. It was *terrible*.'

'Absent fathers,' Stanley said to the sky, as he started strolling down the empty street to where it narrowed and joined the main road – people, cars and mopeds could be seen hurrying to get somewhere.

'The world is full of them.'

Continental Shift, Turkey

1

Customs officer at the Port of Izmir,
with his cocky cap, motorway-cop sunglasses

and bushy black moustache à la Atatürk,
was either vaguely threatening

or vaguely Village People. Kept expecting him
to launch into a Turkish version of 'YMCA',

break into a butch line-formation dance
(could use that gun in its holster as mike).

Instead, he raised his hand for us to stop,
directing us to pull up/engine off.

Smile and act friendly, I'd warned Stanley,
as we edged our way off the Blue Star Ferry

behind a juddering line-up of juggernauts
(what wouldn't pass their MOT back in Blighty).

'Can't believe we're here,' he yawned,
stretching out in his seat like he'd done

nothing more strenuous than sleep
the entire journey, jammy bugger that he is.

'Course, I'd planned on a Greek Island like Crete,
but the boats from Ancona were stalled –

a strike, they said, no end in sight, they said –
so we headed to the port of Venice in the north

and found ourselves bound for a country
neither had visited before: the Republic of Turkey.

2

Was getting nearer to that wayward son of mine
who'll either hug me with surprised arms or . . .

Not a day goes by but I don't dream of him –
he's on a raft and I'm on the rescuing ship.

What can he do but climb aboard,
forgive the mum who gave him everything,

who couldn't bear to see him leave –
the only thing she'd ever called her own.

'Off to seek my fortune,' he'd said.
'In a sea full of stingrays and pirahnas,' I spat back.

Look, he were only sixteen. I was counting
on his company another five years at least.

He'd save on rent, bills, food, clothes,
and, to be honest, he'd no idea how to tidy

his own mess, wash his own smalls,
make a decent sandwich or even his own bed –

so how was he going to manage living
at the farthest ends of the known world

without his personal secretary, housemaid,
chef, financial adviser and chief exec?

3

That customs officer fingered my black
United Kingdom passport at length,

glancing up to compare information to person,
as if he couldn't quite believe . . . something.

When he asked for our vehicle documents,
my lips went dry, armpits moist,

and I was thrown back to Dover the morning
they strip-searched both me and my motor,

yes, my clothes and my holes and poor Matilda's
winter coat, thermals and mechanical undergarments,

when every other sod, native and foreign,
sailed through; yet I, a law-abiding Englishwoman,

was prohibited from entering my own country
for four hours before they let me go.

If I were a drug baron, I'd wanted to spit out,
I'd send my stash with the doddery blue-rinses

and the 2.5 blue-eyed picture-perfect families,
so look to them, you blinking wallies!

4

When the Black Power Movement jetted
across the Atlantic, made an emergency

landing outside my council flat in Chapeltown,
when I were in my twenties and desperate

to swing with the Sixties, it brought a shipment
of unprocessed hair in the shape of an Afro,

the shocking slogan Black is Beautiful
and a longing for 'Our African Culture',

which my BPM mates from the Caribbean,
with their kente cloth headscarves and stick-insect

Masai-goat-herder-sculptures-on-the-sideboard,
said was my *authentic* one. But the only culture I knew

wrapped greasy chips in dirty old newspaper
with battered fish and squashed peas,

and better the devil you know anyway.
Africa's a continent, not a country,

so which of its cultures, thousands of tribes
and languages is mine, exactly?

I told them to cut the crap and go emigrate there,
'cos it's cheaper and warmer than Blighty,

then you'll not have to endure such longing for it.
Whereupon they cussed me off as a sad case

of coconut-itis and angrily broke off all contact.
Look, I may have a cantankerous obeah woman

buried not so deeply in my genetic code,
but I'm a Yorkshire woman, and reet proud of it.

So when this customs man said,
'*Günaydin*, do you have anything to declare?'

I caged my carnivorous, throat-ripping beasts
that'd land me in prison should I let them out,

stopped myself replying, 'Ten kilos of heroin,
stolen Roman antiquities and a crate full of AK47s'

and mouthed 'NO', smiling lasciviously,
thrusting my breasts and fluttering, yes, fluttering.

(Had to shoot Stanley a look when I heard
him almost fail to suppress a fit of giggles.)

What is the purpose of your visit?
'We're on an extended motoring holiday, sweetheart.'

Whipped off his wraparounds at that, exposing
blood-veined eye-whites, stroked his mussie slowly

and asked my cleavage, quite brazenly,
You born 1941? 'Yes, love.' *No, really?*

'A woman would never add years to her age.'
You must born America. Chicken George!

Cosby Show! Michael Jackson! Have a nice day-ay!
'Guess again,' I purred.

You Jamaican? Bob Marley? I shot the sheriff,
Get up, stand up. No woman no . . .

'No Jamaican.' *Moroccan?* 'No Moroccan.'
Ah, Brazilian! Pele best footballer in the world –

one thousand two hundred goals – not out!
Eng-*lish*,' I said, as if proffering a kiss. *Really?*

'York-*shire* to be precise.' I kissed up my shire
as I'd done my lish, lusciously, tempted to suggest

he actually read the damned passport,
seeing as he'd spent ages looking at it.

Just then another officer barked an order
at my attentive new suitor to hurry us along.

You have nice holiday in Turkey, Yorkshire lass.
See you later, alligator! he sing-songed out,

standing to attention and saluting.
'In a while, crocodile,' I sing-songed back,

as we drove out of the port to an exclamation
in perfectly pronounced patois – *Raaastafari!*

The Silken Road

Izmir – where the Silk Road met the sea. Caravans of camels brought carpets, conquest and colours; they brought cosmetics, costumes and calligraphy; Stanley lugged Clasford all the way from London, Clasford who was settling inside him now;

crenallated stone walls enclosed wheat and barley plantations; there were orange, lemon and grapefruit orchards; tomato and cotton fields; cattle, goats, sheep; butternut squashes were sold at the roadside, and cabbages the size of a woman at full term, and red pomegranates split open to reveal their slippery, succulent seeds;

they drove through a village narrowly avoiding a skipping, squealing flurry of orange and green embroidered butterflies; men wearing white shirts and black woollen waistcoats sat on squat stools – they all had black moustaches and some wore flat caps – they all had lived-in features, scooped out like lino cuts; women stood in door-ways, children sucking thumbs clasped their mother's billowy floral trousers; they all stopped talking – it was as if they'd never seen a car before; it was just so quiet there, two foreigners driving through, and everyone was waving and everything was new;

Stanley commented, 'We're peeping voyeurs'; Jessie replied, 'No, we're simply voyagers';

they parked up alongside a khaki river sprinkled with the dandruff of poplars; found a spot where a lattice of grape vines looped around string nets; the ceremonious breaking of bread and cheese, with olives, with figs; bow-legged women with soggy, paper-bag faces approached with dragging feet, selling honey, fruit, bread;

Stanley's head lay in Jessie's lap; she stroked his brow, neutralizing the electrons of his nervous system, sunlight stippling his face through the lattice; he told her about Clasford's last years, how his father drank hope into oblivion and welcomed the death-catcher; how his son tried to care for him; how he tried to recall fond memories of his father – was there even one afternoon spent at the swings in the park? A game of *Monopoly*? A trip to see West Ham play? A man-to-man over a beer in a pub?;

she reassured him that he needn't worry about a thing, while he was with her; before she could hold her tongue, she said that at least having a father who was a burden was better than no father at all;

he sat up, suggested they move along;

there were clouds in rush-hour collision, clouds on go-slow; there were straw tepees in fields; marble graves built like Victorian cradles; in wooded dells there were rows of white boxes collecting honey; in forests there were trees with the bony legs and flat chests of children;

the countryside doesn't change as much as cities do, Stanley observed aloud;

they brought saffron, spices, sperm, slaves, silver, stories, ivory, songs; they wore gems and germs; they traded gunpowder, gold, glass; Jessie brought the convent from high up in the hills of Leeds, it was the stone mansion with which she had been clad, the task of excavation awaited her; Stanley brought the visitors who'd come and gone, yet still lingered on;

they brought religion and refugees, ideas and medicine, myths and music, melanin by the caravan-load; Stanley brought Pearline and a love that would never die; Jessie brought a longing for her son that just wouldn't bloody abate; they brought war and water, perfume and porcelain, politics and poems, peace and paper; Stanley wore loss and brought hope; Jessie wore loss and brought humour;

they both brought mourning for the death of childhood, memories that would not fade;

and there was silk too – Japan, Korea, China, Pakistan, Afghanistan, Tajikistan, Uzbekistan, Turkmenistan, Iran, Azerbaijan, Turkey, Egypt, Italy – this was the Silk Road;

they camped next to the ruins of fortresses and monasteries; *han* – caravanserais, *han* – a safe resting place for Silk Roaders; Stanley willed Alexander the Great to saunter out of the ruins, to regale him with tales of travel and conquest, or Tamerlane, and why not Genghis Khan or Marco Polo, come on, guys, he thought, bring it on; they slept in the car – in the morning they were surrounded by cows;

> One day a Chinese queen accidentally
> dropped a silkworm cocoon into her hot cup of tea.
> As she plucked it out, it unravelled a shiny, silken thread.

they passed petrol stations and pylons; everything was hushed, everything was new and, for a short while, they were listened to their own breathing.

Letter from the Court of Jessie at Ölüdeniz

Dear Me,

Jessie sits like the Queen of Tonga on her foam-backed throne, those fake plaits tied up like a pot plant, natural bushy hair pushing through underneath. Her plaits keep moulting. Sometimes I see one on the ground, a charred worm. She's wearing an African-style wrapper, tied over her breasts, that falls just below her knees. Her legs flap open as she sits. I've told her it is *not* ladylike. I favour a pair of cut-off jeans and show off my sunken chest. Oh, I know all the girls are secretly going wild.

Ölüdeniz Camping is Turkey's best-kept secret, tucked away behind a lagoon. It's reached via a winding road from the main beach, which arcs towards mountains spread with shrubs, like blankets of bobble-stitch. The main beach has a family hotel, a couple of bars, some bungalows, a grocery store. Here at camp there are six, one-roomed log cabins, camping ground and a tiny stretch of sand strewn with rocks. On the other side of the lagoon is a sandy peninsula where, hidden behind trees, the 'dreaded tourists' descend every day to sunbathe.

Cabin Number 4 has been the centre of Court all summer. One bed on each side with our luggage underneath. It's positioned in front of a path of hardened earth lined with eucalyptus trees that provide shade. The lagoon swells a few feet away. It should be paradise.

Friedrich, a computer engineer, and Christa, his housewife, are the first to arrive for an audience at Court this Saturday evening. A rather bovine middle-aged couple, they've driven their mobile home (size of a coach) all the way from Hanover. There are metal bars on the windows, a monster fridge full of Becks and Holsten and a freezer stuffed with frozen German vegetables, meat and *Milch*. Their Alsatian, Caligula, sits unleashed outside their door until they return.

They bring eight cans of lager, and laugh at every single joke Jessie cracks.

Gülten and Yelmen, retired schoolteachers from Marmaris, are next. They position themselves as guests of honour on each side of the throne. They've been coming to this spot ever since it was a farmer's field used by hippies that the Magic Bus took from London to India for a dose of spiritual enlightenment, man. Yeah, like, groovy. I can't imagine these two as the hashish-smoking hippies they claim they were, but I guess most people do get more staid as they get older, everything fixed rigid: their opinions, hearts, their lifestyles. Look at me – Stan the Philosopher, the one who broke free.

Tonight they bring *burma kadayif* – shredded wheat with pistachios and honey. Gülten smiles at Jessie's lip-smacking delight, then shakes her head with what can only be described as pity when I decline, as always, her little diabetic bombs of sugars.

Every morning I go to the camp shop and buy some bread and milk. I then watch Jessie eat half a Turkish loaf oozing chocolate spread while I make a fresh fruit salad. She must have put on over a stone. Next, I air my bedding, and hers. I don't want to share bed bugs.

The two Alexs: young and old, fat and thin, hairy and bereft of, are newcomers. Jessie met them on the beach yesterday. They wear black signet rings and speak of the hardships they escaped in the USSR. Now living in New York, they buy kilims, alabaster carvings and meerschaum pipes shaped into turbaned pashas for their Eastern Eye shop on Fifth Avenue.

They bring a bottle of vodka and a box of Ferrero Rocher chocolates for Jessie. She thanks them with an exuberant performance of 'Bali Ha'i', again.

The three university students from Rotterdam scuttle over: Toos, Wieneke and Anja, who want a bit of Turkish, and get it most nights at the Turkish Delights Disco on the main beach. They bring roll-ups, hangovers, caustic wine and girly gossip.

The highlight of my week is going to the bazaar in Fethiye. I've become rather proficient at haggling. While Jessie is brought a stool, mint *çay* in a miniature glass and invariably an offer of marriage by some balding market trader, I wander between sacks of beans, nuts, barley and the most dazzling array of spices known to man, exercising my favourite Turkish words: *Çok pahali* – very expensive.

The Cow Lady, who won't give her name, submerged in layers and scarves, tends cows in the grazing ground up the road. She says to Jessie, 'You *güzel*', and nods at me to concur. I was reading *Bleak House* from my Complete Works of Dickens one afternoon when she picked it up, weighed it in her hand and decided with much gravity, 'This, good book.' She brings the exoticism of having a *real peasant* in our midst, as well as a sack of oranges, which she dumps at Jessie's feet.

My nemesis-in-waiting is Sunita from Tooting Bec. She's on her way to India, where she wants to find her roots, and arrived a month ago intending to stay a weekend – the longest one in history. She recites poems by someone called Audre Lorde to Jessie, who milks it. Sunita has pitched her tent directly opposite our cabin and gives me the evil eye. When I complain, I'm brushed off with 'She's harmless. A nice kid. Don't be such a spoilsport.'

Sunita brings a half-drunk bottle of raki, slurred speech and a hopeless crush.

The Court sits in a semicircle around the throne. They are enraptured by anecdotes about army bases in Germany, Rod's little scam, Nancy Pants in working men's clubs, the time Matilda was flooded out to sea in Spain, with Jessie clinging on to the roof rack.

Osman, a restaurant owner from Ankara, has a mop of curly black hair and wears shorts and yellow Wellington boots. He brings a red rose for Jessie between his teeth and she sings 'Summertime' for him. *Summertime and the living is excruciating. Fish are drooling and my lover's on her high horse.* I should know the words inside out by now.

I have a bottle of raki myself, which I'm quickly depleting. It's secreted under my chair.

When we arrived, Jessie became a social hit and she's been riding the wave ever since. I'm sure my ghosts have been scared off by the noise. Every day is showtime. What a difference to Spain. We begin with pleasantries exchanged after breakfast, when she goes on walkabout, and end with these gatherings. I sometimes wonder if it's all an act to show me how everyone thinks she's wonderful. Or are they her emotional bodyguard, protecting her from getting close to me again?

As they gather around tonight, it sinks in that it's not a court at all: they are Followers of the Cult of St Jessie. (And I hope she'll lead them in a mass suicide one day soon.)

Somehow, we've slid back. If I take too long at the toilet, she no longer looks anxious but askance. Even so, I feign constipation on a regular basis. This prompts her to feed me soaked prunes. When I feign an allergy to them, she buys senna pods from the bazaar.

St John, pronounced 'Sinjun' (as he tells everybody), went to Eton and Oxford (as he tells everybody) and is a scientist for Glaxo in Istanbul (as he tells everybody), pausing to monitor the impact. He brings with him the British Class System, and his boyfriend, Muhammad.

We have what is called a transient population here. Antipodeans, Scandinavians, Americans, all manner of western Europeans and Yugoslavs. Sometimes there're as many as twenty paying homage.

Oh, and there's someone else here too. Whatsisname? Ah, yes, I know, that nondescript little fellow called Stanley, sitting out of the loop and getting quietly sozzled.

Night is now seeping into my pores. The lagoon and sky have turned the shade of violet last seen in the young Elizabeth Taylor's eyes in *Cleopatra*. The eucalyptus trees above suddenly look like blurred willow trees that should be hanging over a swamp. Bats begin to swoop from one tree to the other. I do my nightly duty by lighting some candles that hang in little baskets from the cabin. The rest of the camp is sitting outside as well, or else they are getting ready to go out. Some are putting young children to bed or letting them run noisily around. The Turkish pop music in the café has just been raised a notch, unfortunately.

I turn back to hear Jessie sounding off about money. About how *we* believe the point of it is to enjoy it today because a bus can run you over tomorrow. It isn't the royal 'we'. It's the cringe-making 'we'. I've put up with it all summer.

'Jessie, I don't agree with you.' I project with the authority of a Shakespearean actor playing King Lear, surprising not only myself. 'Yes, spend and enjoy money within limits, but I believe it's also important to save and invest for the future. It's a universal law that like attracts like, if you see what I mean. Making money out of money is a way to build wealth –'

'Hey,' she interjects, 'you're not in the boring old bank now, so chill out.'

Everyone laughs. The raki is burning me up.

'Well, as I'm the one who's bankrolled our extended Turkish sojourn and therefore provided this great opportunity for you underlings to sit with the Queen of Tonga, I think it's about time you brought me some gifts too.'

I have to say, it's my Ground Swallowing Stanley Moment, which I have to style out or else go walk in the lagoon with two rocks tied to my feet. So I look from one to another, as if to intimidate, starting with Jessie, who looks outraged.

There is silence.

Gülten and Yelmen each put an arm around her shoulders in solidarity. Friedrich looks somewhat proud, as if I'd finally spoken up for the whole of mankind. Christa shakes her head, as if she despaired of the whole of mankind. The two Alexs seem to have just noticed me for the first time, and young Alex is giving me the eye. I'm almost sure of it. The Dutchies give me the kind of filthy look that demotes me to something excremental moulded into human form. The Cow Lady, picking up on the atmosphere, puts her hands to her chest in horror, as if I've just confessed to sullying a village full of virgin girls. Sinjun shouts, 'Oh, drama, drama! Have we got an umpire?' And so on.

Sunita takes the opportunity to sit on her intended's lap and force Jessie's arms around her, until Osman, humming a waltz, grabs a grateful Jessie by the hand and pulls her up into a dance, sending Sunita crashing to the floor.

Jessie says over her shoulder, 'If it wasn't for me, he'd still be listening to garden sprinklers every Saturday evening.'

The oracle has spoken.

I go into the cabin with as much insouciance as I can muster, and slam the door.

Wish I were somewhere else

Love,
Whatsisname?

Summer of 1989: Court Budget

Dear Jessie,

MONTHLY EXPENDITURE

Description	Amount
Rental of log 'palace'	£32.00
Food	£30.00
Feeding the 5,000	£10.00
Provisions	£5.00
Alcohol	£4.00
Toiletries	£5.00
Calor gas	£6.00
Petrol	£3.00
Women's Magazines	£2.50
Cappuccinos	£5.00
Lovely trips to historic sites	£0.00
Dolmus rides	£0.00
Cinema	£0.00
Postcards/ postage	£0.00
Miscellaneous (*cakes*, etc.)	£7.50
Total Monthly Expenditure	**£110.00**

INCOME

Stanley's credit card	£110.00
Gainful or otherwise employment	£Zilch
Total Monthly Income	**£110.00**

Analysis: Stanley is at the end of his tether

Signature: *Stanley Orville Cleve Williams*, B.Sc. (Quant)

Stanley, dear

REAL BUDGET NOT FANTASY ONE

Love (unconditional)	£REE!
Complete loyalty	£REE!
Mothering	£REE!
Friendship	£REE!
Sunshine	£REE!
Conversation	£REE!
Laughter	£REE!
Initiative	£REE!
Adventure	£REE!
Therapist (savings)	£REE!
Social life/entertainment	£REE!
Cook's wages	£REE!
Motivational speeches	£REE!
Purchase of vehicle	£REE!

INCOME

Jessie	1,000%
Total Monthly Income	**£NCALCULABLE!**

Advice: Be grateful for life's blessings

Signature: *Jessie O'Donnell*, Ph.D. Univ. Hrd Knks (Orphan)

Dreams of a Faraway Place

Dear Jessie,

By the time you wake up, I will be on my way to Istanbul. Fear not, I am only going for a few days. I *will* be back soon. You know I've not been myself for a while now, so I am hoping to return refreshed and better company for you. Enclosed is some lira to see you through until I get back.

All I can say is that I need some, yes, I know it's a dirty word, space.

Yours as ever
Stanley

A Trip Down Memory Lane

Tread of trainers on earth. Rustle of a leaf disturbed by a mild gust. Trickle of light on dusty bushes. Yellow flower of the chrysanthemum, drooped. Mudded wheel ruts made by campsite traffic after rain. A termite mound at the base of a tree was an eroded terracotta pot. A chain gang of track-laying ants crossed his passage – destroyed. Exposed nerve antennae at the back of his neck. The dreaded hand on his shoulder: 'Where do you think *you're* going, Sneaky Stanley?'

Out on to the empty beach of Ölüdeniz. Sand sucked up waves like an asthmatic devouring oxygen. Two fishermen staggered up the beach under the weight of baskets of fish that threatened to topple them. Turned left to walk up the mountain, past a sunken grove littered with oranges so ripe they were rotten. A few isolated stone cottages secreted in between trees. Then rose, steeply, rose into morning. Turned back to see the beach so far down below that waves dashing the shore were white race horses competing at the finishing line. Reached the top, out of breath, the road deserted in both directions. A scarecrow crucified in a field; in the distance a lone whitewashed bungalow with wire rods sticking out of the flat roof.

During the climb Stanley's mind began to shed its debris. By the time he arrived at the top, he felt lighter. He sat down on a boulder at the bus stop.

For the first time in months he was looking forward to something.

The dolmuş rolled up, packed with elderly women wearing long dresses and shawls, bearing baskets to sell at market, and backpackers departing early for their next destination. The only seat available was next to a stout woman whose crinkled brown hair was tied into a loose bun, topped by a straw hat trimmed with lemon- and lime-coloured petals. He scanned the pearl earrings, coral necklace, the unusual jade dress flared at the sleeves, beribboned at the waist. She lifted her skirts to make room for him.

'Come sit, dahling. Constantinople is a long way away and we want you to be cosy.'

So is Kathmandu and Timbuktu, Stanley thought, before replying, 'I'm only going as far as Istanbul, actually.'

His companion chuckled. 'Constantinople and Istanbul are one and the same, although the former is the parent of the latter.'

Intrigued, he studied her profile under the guise of looking out of the window. She seemed ageless, blessed with a prettiness suffused with the kind of dignity not bestowed at birth but that one had to earn.

'Would you like an apple?'

My mother told me never to accept gifts from strangers, he almost quipped, before nodding his assent. He had had no breakfast.

'It is true. I am a stranger,' she replied, even though he had not spoken aloud. Or had he?

On her lap was a basket covered with a white napkin. She withdrew the type of small, hard, flawed fruit he hadn't seen since his childhood. It didn't look like plastic, nor did it taste watery.

'I have been making this trip every summer for as long as I can remember. This part of the world is very dear to my heart. In the winter I fly home to Jamaica, to be with my mother.'

Stanley had thought her accent familiar, and he now recognized it as the genteel lilt of Jamaica's middle classes: that subtle inflection that the mother country's schoolteachers could never iron out completely. His parents would mock her as *one-a dose hoity-toity Uptown Browns*.

'My parents are Jamaican too. Rather, they were.' He felt so comfortable with this woman that he became more chatty than he'd been in months. 'I'm always recalling things they used to say. Sometimes I can hardly separate their thoughts from mine; they just jump in and deliver some opinion or wisdom. Much the same as they did in life.'

'That is the Jamaican way, as you know.'

'Do I? I don't really. I'm a Londoner and, well, it might sound pretentious, but these days a citizen of the world, so to speak, or of Europe at least. Hey, maybe we're related.'

'I very much doubt it, my dear, unless your parents lived to be two hundred years old.'

She turned to look at him directly for the first time. Her eyes glistened like spoonfuls of raw demerara sugar; yet they had no soft centre – no pupils. He sunk into his seat and slapped his forehead with his palm and exclaimed, 'Bomboclaat!'

'And if you wish to converse with me, kindly refrain from such profanities. I am sure your father did not raise you to talk like that.'

Just as Stanley was going to reply that his father would slap him upside his head if ever he spoke a hint of the patois that his father spoke all the time, she continued. 'My father was an army officer from Scotland. I never did meet him, but I am proud of my Scotch blood. Now, my Creole mother was a free woman, a doctress, who kept a boarding house on East Street in Kingston, and it was she who passed on the science of herbs and midwifery that had been handed down by the slaves. This I supplemented with the medical knowledge taught me by the European doctors.'

'May I ask your name, ma'am?' He did not know where the ma'am came from, but it seemed appropriate.

'You may. I am Mrs Mary Jane Seacole.' Her tone was somewhat self-reverential. 'Indeed, the very one. Yes, I am she.'

He thought of feigning recognition, but he'd concluded very early on in life that lying was ultimately a very stressful exercise. Not the actual lying itself but maintaining the pretence.

'Should I have heard of you, Mary?'

He immediately knew he should have, because she delivered the kind of fruity, rubbery *tchups!* more associated with a Trenchtown market trader than with an Uptown Brown.

'Mek I tell you somet'ing. During my time *everyone* had heard of me, and so they will again. And, you must kindly call me Mrs Seacole, young man.'

She then regained her composure as if she had never dropped it, lifted a corner of the napkin and brought out a brittle, antique book. This she passed over.

'Be careful or it will come apart. It is the first edition of my autobiography, *The Wonderful Adventures of Mrs Seacole in Many*

Lands, and it is exactly one hundred and thirty-two years old this very day.'

An older, hardened, more masculine Mrs Seacole was pictured on the cover. Stanley likened her to a rakish buccaneer, with her wide-brimmed black hat tilted back at an angle, a neckerchief, a black doublet.

'You wrote this?' He ran his hands over the book.

'Is that not me on the front? I was most famous after the war, most famous. I received many medals of honour.'

'I guess I should have heard of you, then, Mrs Seacole. That's me all over. I know nothing.'

'Allow me to elucidate. It all began when my husband, Edward Horatio Nelson, godson of Lord Nelson, of whom you are no doubt familiar, passed away shortly after our marriage. Unfortunately tragedy struck twice.'

She took the book out of his hand and read aloud, '*I had one other grief to master, the loss of my mother, and then I was allowed to battle with the world as best I might.*'

'I understand grief,' Stanley said, almost to himself; it was private, not to be talked about without a great deal of pain.

'You will be able to talk freely about your parents in time. When there is more distance.'

'Yeah, right, like two hundred years?' he snapped, unable to censor either his thoughts or his words with this woman.

'If it takes that long, so be it,' she snapped back. 'And, by the way, *you* are a very impertinent young man.'

'Sorry. My mind's not my own these days.' He raised an eyebrow at her.

Mrs Seacole continued to read. '*As I grew into womanhood, I began to indulge that longing to travel which will never leave me while I have health and vigour. I was never weary of tracing upon an old map the route to England; and never followed with my gaze the stately ships homeward bound without longing to be in them, and see the blue hills of Jamaica fade into the distance.*' Looking out of the window, she viewed the landscape of barren rocks for the longest while.

Stanley attempted to bring her round. 'I'm a traveller now. I don't know where I'll end up, but the ride can be so exhilarating. It's like I'm walking on a map of the world and the white cliffs of Dover have faded into memory.' He'd never seen the white cliffs of Dover, but it was a romantic image and it worked. She turned back to him.

'A little suffering is necessary, because it can make us search our souls very, very deeply.'

'Isn't life funny like that?' he blurted out, for want of anything more meaningful to say.

'No, it is not,' she reprimanded. 'Life is a very serious matter. Especially when it no longer fills you up from the inside, but has abandoned you to watch it as an observer who can sympathize but no longer empathize.

'Now, let me continue. How I longed to escape the suffocating restraints of slave society in Jamaica. As soon as it was possible, I left, even though I knew that as a woman travelling alone I eschewed respectability in the eyes of my countrymen. In Panama, where I was fondly known as Aunty Seacole or the Yellow Doctress, I tended cholera victims, surviving all manner of hoodlum nonsense and the ghastly disease itself. I had previously tended the English on Jamaica who were dying from yellow fever. Those poor unfortunates had little resistance to it.'

He interrupted her flow: 'How could you help those who were there to profit from slavery? They were the lowest form of humanity.'

'While I do not have to explain myself to you, I will tell you this: it was my duty as a healer to help those who needed me. And you are a very judgemental person, I do believe.'

As Stanley had never been accused of this before, he was taken aback. Was she right? Instant appraisal, instant dismissal? Had he been wrong about Alessandro? Was he really just like his father? Lashing out with his thoughts, if not always his tongue? Was he judgemental about Jessie? Was no one ever good enough for him? Was he just a self-righteous prig?

Mrs Seacole took his hands in hers and rubbed them. They did not pass through him. Here, he thought, is a woman of substance.

'Stanley,' she said.

Of course she would know his name.

'You are too hard on yourself. It is easier to understand life on earth when you are no longer concerned about your own survival.'

He rested his head against her shoulder as he had done with Pearline, until, that is, Clasford told her that if she continued to mollycoddle him, she would make a woman out of his son. One more file catalogued against his father in his huge library of resentments. No wonder he had been so unhappy. It was time to burn the library to the ground.

'In 1854 I heard about the Crimean War and a passion to embark on that lengthy journey lodged itself in my heart and would not budge. I set sail for England and made many applications to the War Office and nursing agencies but without success. I sought out Florence Nightingale's office, where I was interviewed by one of her staff.' Mrs Seacole picked up her book and began to read. *'And I saw in her face the fact that, had there been a vacancy, I should not have been chosen to fill it.*

'And one cold evening I stood in the twilight . . . did these ladies shrink from accepting my aid because my blood flowed beneath a somewhat duskier skin than theirs? Tears streamed down my foolish cheeks, as I stood in the fast thinning streets; tears of grief that anyone should doubt my motives.

'What do you think I did, young Stanley? Why, I sent myself, did I not? I shall not dwell on the vicissitudes of my travels except to say that the journey took me to Gibraltar, Malta, on to Constantinople, and thereon by boat to Scutari, where I was most excited at the prospect of finally meeting Miss Nightingale. When I arrived at her hospital, safely behind the trenches, her secretary eyed me with much surprise. *Miss Nightingale has the entire management of our hospital staff, but I do not think that any vacancy* . . .

'I stood my ground, so they eventually had to take me to meet her. *A slight figure in the nurse's dress; with a pale, gentle, and withal firm face.* She asked what I wanted. I requested a bed for the night and the chance to offer my services to the sick. The former was granted. The latter denied. *I would have worked for the wounded, for bread and water.*

'Did I turn back? I tell you, *fer true*, Mrs Seacole here had a job of work to do and a job of work she would do. The very next day I crossed the Black Sea to Balaclava, where I was met with the sight of hundreds of wooden boats shuttling back and forth carrying the dead and the wounded. It was an awful sight to behold. Some of the soldiers recognized me from their postings in Jamaica and we exchanged greetings. It was not long before I had overseen the building of the British Hotel at Spring Hill with my business partner, a Mr Day. It was a clean haven for invalids. I dispensed medicines and toured the campsites at the Front, where the soldiers were treated as the loved sons of Mother Seacole.

'Do you know what was written of me in the distinguished *Punch* magazine? Oh, I will tell you.

> *'That berry-brown face, with a kind heart's trace*
> *Impressed on each wrinkle sly*
> *Was a sight to behold, through the snow-clouds rolled*
> *Across that iron sky'*

'You must have been a genuine trailblazer, Mrs Seacole. A tour de force, a veritable rocket of tenacity, a Messianic –'

'Yes, yes,' she interrupted with impatience. 'Do I detect a tendency on your part to hyperbole, or perhaps you are mocking me because you are a very impertinent person? For myself it was straightforward – I was following the Good Lord's calling. I was simply doing my duty.'

'My girlfriend Jessie, the one who brought me here, as she keeps reminding me. Well, she imagines herself an adventurer.'

'Did your friend carry you on her back?'

He laughed. 'She'd say so, metaphorically speaking.'

'Nonsense! You brought yourself here and you gave her the companionship and support she needed to undertake this journey.'

This was the opening he needed. He jumped in and began to sound off, counting with his fingers. 'She's like a benevolent dictator, got to be the centre of attention, doesn't listen to me, got to do things her way –'

'Would you be on this trip if she had listened to you? If I had listened to people, I would never have left my tiny island.'

'You don't understand. No opinion counts but her own. I can't even go to the loo without getting a grilling. It's a nightmare!'

'If it's a nightmare, may I ask why you remain with her? Surely you are with her because it is your choice. Therefore you must stop complaining.'

'I don't know why I'm with her any more!'

There, he'd blurted it out. He knew it was a betrayal.

'But I can't just leave because I'm sort of committed. Not married, we don't bother with that much these days.'

'I am fully aware of your society's mores and lack of morals, young man. You must answer me this: if your father were alive, would you be here now?'

'No way. I would never have contemplated leaving, even before he needed my help. He'd have called me a vagabond, a waster.'

'My mother would have wanted me in Jamaica too. If she had lived longer, I would never have had such a remarkable life. Ask yourself this question: if I stay with this Jessie, what will I be like in ten years' time?'

He hesitated, although the answer required no meditation.

'Crushed,' he mumbled.

'To be avoided, is it not?'

She smiled at him for the first time since they'd met, as if she'd accomplished what she had set out to achieve. She had no teeth. Her mouth was a black hole. Stanley tried not to stare.

'I think you were way ahead of your time, Mrs Mother Aunty Yellow Doctress Mary Jane Seacole.'

'I do believe you are correct, you impudent rapscallion. It is truly of some sadness to me that I was not born in your time.' She sighed, rubbing her chest. 'Do you know that after the war a fund was set up for me by Crimean veterans who wrote to the very distinguished *Times* newspaper rallying support for me? *While the benevolent deeds of Florence Nightingale are being handed down to posterity with blessings and imperishable renown, are the actions of Mrs Seacole to be entirely forgotten?* A Grand Military Festival benefit was held for me over four nights at the Royal Surrey Gardens. It was attended by forty thousand people. Oh, my dear, I was lionized, my boy, I was *lionized.*'

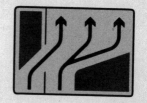

Old Istanbul

Last stop! Büyük Charsi! Last stop! Büyük Charsi!

I crawled out of sleep to no Mother Seacole,
and a deserted bus. I stepped on to

a slag heap of bloated beans, fish spines,
bloody bones, pulped fruit, broken eggs,

surrounded by scavengers in red smocks.
I headed towards some market arches,

avoiding dogs chasing each other, rats
dangling from foaming jaws like wet rags.

Under arcaded ceilings, boys carried hillocks
of sweetmeats on their heads; craftsmen

made samovars, cribs, clocks, carpets;
a street seller clinked two cups together,

packages of sherbet in his wooden waist-trough;
cross-legged men sat in coffee shops.

Something was driving me on.
I was thinking *Star Trek*, I was

thinking *Doctor Who*, I was thinking
Voyage to the Bottom of the Sea.

A group of veiled women glided
by in glittering slippers with curled-up toes;

a beggarly man was banging a drum;
rich boppas wore turbans the size of pumpkins,

gems stuck in the middle, jewel-encrusted
daggers hooked into cumbersome belts.

It was Ali Baba & the Forty Thieves.
It was A Thousand & One Nights.

It was Sinbad, Aladdin. Lord, it was bedlam.
It was bizarre. It was the bazaar.

It was the Great Market of Constantinople –
the capital of the Ottoman Empire.

Eighteenth-century Slave Market

The Chief Eunuch of the Palace had been captured and castrated by Egyptian Christians when he was a five-year-old boy in the Sudan. Thirty-five years later he had risen to one of the highest positions in the Ottoman Empire. This morning his white, tubular hat that added fourteen inches to his inconsiderable height, his sumptuous indigo robes that padded out his already rotund shape, his entourage of servants and officials, his sullen obduracy and chilling power, were rewarded with the parting of the crowds on his periodic visit to the slave market.

He had come to view a handsome, dark-skinned Abyssinian boy, who, he had been told, would be a perfect addition to the seraglio.

Stanley had exited the Great Market at Nurosmaniye Gate and charged on until he ended up at Constantine's Column, where he found himself attending a real live slave market.

'What is your name?' the Chief Eunuch demanded of the boy.

'Menelik,' he replied.

The Chief Eunuch slapped the boy in the face. He did not budge or cry.

'Your name is Ibrahim. Do not forget it. What is your name?'

'Menelik,' the boy repeated and, very slowly, rotated his head until his defiant glare landed on Stanley, who was so shocked that he froze. Before his eyes the boy then metamorphosed into an imposing man in military uniform, several medals pinned to his chest, thick, black hair combed flat upon his head but left to curl up over his ears. He was so commanding that Stanley almost felt obliged to attempt an amateurish salute.

'Not a man to mess with,' said a voice behind him. Stanley spun around. 'Hard as nails, that one.'

The owner of the voice was a short man with frizzy hair, olive skin and blue eyes. There was a noticeable moulding of the map of Africa in his rodent-like features, which were encroached upon by bushy sideburns. Leaning against a pillar, he looked debonair and cocky rather than handsome. Out of his black frock coat peeked a white collar, like little wings.

Stanley did not know which one to look at when Menelik/ Ibrahim walked swiftly towards him, chest thrust out, back erect as that of an army officer.

'While you have little else to do with your time, time waits for no man,' he said on his approach. 'I suggest you seize this opportunity to join me on a tour of the seraglio, so that your visit to Constantinople will have been worth while.'

He stood before Stanley with his hands behind his back, feet planted solidly on the ground.

'Major-General Ibrahim Gannibal,' he said, introducing himself, extending a hand; Stanley all but wilted under its iron grip. 'So named by my godfather Tsar Peter the Great, after Hannibal, the Carthaginian general.'

He clearly meant to impress and he did. Stanley felt himself diminish, until Ibrahim looked over Stanley's shoulder and, with a mischievous gleam in his eye, added, 'I don't have to invite *you*. You never stop hanging on to my coat-tails.'

'I am merely carrying out research, Grandad, as well you know.'

'So you keep telling me, Alexander, for the novel you began in 1827, *The Negro of Peter the Great*. It would have been a masterpiece, had you the wherewithal to complete it and guarantee my posthumous glory alongside yours. One cannot turn a corner in the whole of Russia without seeing *another* statue of you in some sort of glamorous pose. Let us recall what was said of you: "Pushkin has a duel almost every day." And, as you yourself wrote after yet another bawdy evening of champagne and actresses: "The former gets drunk and the latter get fucked."'

Smiling to himself, Stanley was aware that this is what he had wished for in a father: a gentle chiding soaked in affection.

'Do you see what I have to put up with, Stanley? I worked damned hard and outgrew the dandyism of my youth, almost. At twenty-one I was already a household name, but Grandad does not understand that my literary ambitions did not die when my body expired at thirty-seven. Oh, though I suspect he is secretly pleased that his great-grandson Alexander Sergeyevich Pushkin is not only considered the father of Russian literature but that he is proud of his Ethiopian roots.'

Pushkin offered Stanley a playful high five, to which Stanley responded with a loud slap that left his palm smarting. He shook it and they both giggled.

'Ah was searchin' for ma roots, Daddy-O!' Pushkin exclaimed in cod American, as he launched into a clumsy attempt to do the Funky Chicken, flapping his arms and trying out some super-slippery footwork. He proceeded to belt out the James Brown hit 'Say it loud! I'm black and I'm proud! Say it loud, I'm black and I'm proud! Yeeeoooowwwww!'

'I love James Brown too,' Stanley managed to say in between bursts of laughter, tempted to join in with this ridiculous impromptu performance.

'Oh woodee-doodee, ain't that coolee. Jimmy's such a crazy cat. Ah go to all his concerts and ah don't pay no dollar, Brother-Stan.'

Ibrahim tutted and raised his eyes with amused tolerance at his great-grandson. 'He has been hanging around those Negro Americans too much, or whatever they call themselves these days. It is, quite frankly, absurd to hear you trying to "get with it" when you are dead.'

Pushkin turned his back on Ibrahim like a spoiled child ostracizing another.

'Grandad knows full well that my mother, Nadezhda Osipovna, acclaimed as "the beautiful creole", was surely the vainest woman in all of Russia and that she hated her middle child – *moi*! – because I alone had inherited something of the old Negro's features, marking me out as pot ugly. She made my childhood hell. When the English artist Dawe wanted to paint me when I was older, I wrote a poem called "Mon Portrait" – it's about how my African profile would last for centuries, only to be mocked by Mephistopheles – and showed it to my mother, telling her this is how she made me feel. Yes, it was all her fault.

'She was so terribly distraught, which was of course my intention. Papa was no better. He had a monstrous temper and was a hopeless womanizer. Then that evil critic Faddei Bulgarin mocked my African grandfather in a literary gazette, to which I replied with the poem "My Genealogy", all about how my black grandfather was close to the Tsar himself. Anyway, is it therefore surprising that I should seek out some black roots? Even if they are American, like your good self.'

'No, I'm British,' Stanley corrected him. 'Of Jamaican parents, I might add.'

'Dammit, Janet! This is so disappointing because those black Americans are just the grooviest people on the planet.'

'Oh, I don't know,' Stanley said, shaking his head. 'Jamaicans are pretty cool too, you know.'

'Sure, brother-man. If I was a Jamaican, I & I woulda been a Rasta, grow natty-dreads an' live ina de hills.'

To his surprise, Stanley found his body spontaneously leaping into an uninhibited skank. He looked comical, with his long, spindly legs and arms sticking out at exaggerated, uncoordinated angles, as he trod the ground in what was supposed to be a rude-bwoy strut to accompany Pushkin's arm-waving oratory.

'I & I woulda worship His Imperial Majesty! Haile Selassie-I! King of Kings! Lord of Lords! Conquering Lion of Judah! Elect of God! Emperor of Ethiopia! I & I –'

'Alexander,' Ibrahim cut in impatiently.

'Yes, Grampy?'

'SHUT-UP!'

'Why should I?' He pulled a truculent face. 'Yu cyan tell I & I wha' fe to do!'

'Of course I can. To use modern parlance, you were a poncey writer during the time of imperial Russia; therefore stop deluding yourself that you could be anything else now.'

'One who suffered the tragedy of childhood. One who was exiled for six years due to the seditious nature of my writing, who thereafter had every word censored by Tsar Nicholas himself.'

'Spare me your self-pity, and let us not compete on the tragedy of childhood because I suspect I will come out as victor. One shoulders it.' He directed his attention to Stanley and said in a matter-of-fact manner, 'I was abducted by a French adventurer who was acquiring a host of unusual objects to put in the ageing Louis XIV's palace of Versailles. Fortunately, fate intervened. I was confiscated by officials in Cairo and sent on to the auction block here, eventually being brought to Tsar Peter by the Russian ambassador.'

'I spent my childhood in total despair!' Pushkin shouted out. 'Total despair! Stanley, do you understand?'

In that moment Stanley saw that the journey from England, with all its characters and happenings, had not only freed him from the bondage of his early years but also opened up the history of his country and continent to him. He rested against the pillar. After skanking so energetically, he was feeling heady. This was the first time he had danced since the Under Sixteens Disco in Tower Hamlets nearly twenty years earlier. It was exhilarating. Why had it taken him so long to get here?

The other two stood watching him, waiting for him to speak.

'I do understand because I too spent my childhood in total despair.' He began quietly, expecting what he'd grown used to with Jessie: for such extrovert personalities to butt in and shift the conversation back to themselves. But he felt such total acceptance emanating from his newfound friends that he became more confident, more animated. 'I was never allowed to play with other children because my father didn't want me running round the streets and ending up in trouble. He never liked my schoolfriends, so I was never allowed into their houses. I was always alone. I longed for adulthood, but when adulthood came, I didn't have a clue about what I wanted out of life. The muscle for making my own decisions hadn't been used, you see. I was just a product of my father's instruction, an automaton. Now I'm not. Now I'm becoming a . . . someone.'

'At least I was lucky to be sent away to the imperial Lyceum, where I could be my own adorable self. I have *always* been a someone.'

'A little suffering helped to make you a good writer, Alexander,' Ibrahim said. 'Fool not thyself. How many artistes grew up without trouble in their hearts? You should be grateful that it was a tough ride and not an easy one.'

Pushkin put an arm around Stanley's shoulders. 'What did I tell you? He's a hard man, with such backhanded compliments. I was merely good, not great.'

He ran his hand over his curls with camp affectation. 'I should have been on *Oprah*, Stanley. She would have adored me, with my artistic triumph over an abusive childhood, low self-esteem and a drink problem. I watch her every day. Do you know her?'

'No, I've not met her,' Stanley said, grinning. 'I'm just an Ordinary Joe, not of the status to mix in showbiz circles.'

'Hush! Well, you do now. *Moi, par exemple.* Come, my new friend, let us follow the Chief Eunuch and his latest acquisition to the seraglio at Topkapi Palace and entertain you some more. This is a treat par excellence. Except for the sultan, no fully equipped men are allowed into this heavenly-hard-on-haven-of-a-harem. It is such a pity that in the netherworld one cannot, you know, satisfy two hundred and fifty frustrated maidens primed in the art of love-making but with so little chance to practise it. In case you're wondering, the motivation does not go but the mechanics are simply *pas possible.*'

There was a recklessness to Pushkin that Stanley liked – the kind of boy he had wanted to befriend at school but who would never bestow friendship upon him. A lively companion from his own peer group, for a change.

Pushkin? Pushkin?

'What books have you written?' he asked, debating whether to pretend to have read them.

In the Sultan's Seraglio

The waters of the Golden Horn, the Sea of Marmara and the Bosporus converged at Seraglio Point, where Topkapi Palace was enclosed within a fortified wall.

The Chief Eunuch, his entourage, the boy Menelik and their invisible followers entered via the Court of Janissaries, where the sultan's elite corp were sitting eating from great cauldrons. They continued on through the Gate of Salutations, through a landscaped garden and finally through the Gate of Felicity and into a labyrinth of blue and turquoise tiles, mosaics, porticoes, recesses, balconies, the mist of fountains. They went through several interlinking rooms around a courtyard, until they came to an airy apartment where women lounged in silks on embroidered cushions, combing each other's long hair, reading, sewing, applying make-up to each other. There was a wispy breathlessness of female voices without the drone of the male bass.

The boy Menelik sat down at the feet of the Valide Sultan, the sultan's mother, who ran the household. Stanley thought her make-up so grotesque that she could have been a pantomime dame.

The three men sat together on a bed of cushions.

'I expected them to be naked,' Stanley whispered to Pushkin, unable to hide his disappointment.

'Hey, brother, you've been watching too many Hollywood films with breast-popping belly-dancing harem girls. Relax, dude. The harem is simply where the women of the household live. This is it. One comes here to soak it up and dream. That crabby harridan the Valide is going to be in my novel about Grandad.'

The boy Menelik was staring into the middle distance.

'Tell me about him, I mean you,' Stanley asked Ibrahim.

'I had been brought in as the Valide's coffee-maker but soon became her favourite. I was always someone's favourite. There were two hundred black eunuchs working in the palace who despised this Abyssinian boy who had been left intact. I had to be alert to danger at all times. I am pleased to report that I was never interfered with.'

'Well, I wish someone would interfere with me,' Pushkin groaned as he did a backroll on to the cushions, threw his legs into the air, then bounced into an upright sitting position again. 'Stanley: do you have a woman to call your own? As the Cockneys say, "Me uvver arf". As the Rastas say, "Mi queen". As the rappers say, "Ma bitch". As the sultans say, "My wives, concubines and anyone else I can lay my hands on".'

'I suppose I do have one and I suppose she is my girlfriend. Jessie. I left her way down south, where we're camping.'

'You lucky thing.' Pushkin punched his arm. 'Is she any good?'

'No, she's bad, actually.'

'Huh! The wicked ones are the best. A real bad-ass *ho*! I am jealous beyond belief.'

'Don't be. She's probably sticking voodoo pins into my effigy as we speak.'

'Why would she do that? Is she a witch?'

'She'd like to be. It's just that I've gone walkabout without getting her signed permission. She treats me like a pet dog.'

'Ah, yes, typical of the conniving sex!' Ibrahim joined in the conversation with surprising enthusiasm. 'I had my first wife imprisoned as an adulteress for five years. Do not look so appalled, Stanley. Women were often consigned to convents if they were unmarried or for some other misdemeanour. This one gave birth to a white baby. I found happiness with my second wife. We had eleven children: nine survived and my son Osip was Alexander's grandfather.'

'Oh, boring, boring. I've heard your stories a thousand times, Grandpa. Now you, Stanley, must not put up with being bossed around by this bad-ass bitch Jessie. Promise me, swear to it.'

'I swear to it,' Stanley replied, placing his arm across his chest, knowing he would honour this oath.

Ibrahim continued, 'It is quite unnerving to come face to face with your childhood self. I can see the boy is unhappy, but I cannot inhabit him.'

'He reminds me of my younger self,' Stanley said. 'Sitting alone, staring into nothingness.'

He saw that Ibrahim understood.

'I wish I were able to reassure the boy Menelik that memories of his nineteen brothers, the wind-swept plateaus and gorges of Abyssinia, *injera* – the bread his mother made every day – the aroma of her musk, how he walked in the maize and millet fields behind his father's three legs, the third being a knobbly walking stick, will not fade completely but with each year become less painful. I wish I could tell him that he will become the favourite of Tsar Peter the Great; that he will pick up the Russian and French tongues as if they were his own; that the Tsar will send him to military school in Paris to study mathematics and engineering, at which he excels; that the Tsar will write asking him to come home to Russia soon, because he misses him; that the boy will outlive six changes of throne and become an important man in the military and government; that he will be happy again.'

'I'd tell my young self this too,' said Stanley. 'Because right now I am happy, here, now, with you guys. I never even knew there were black people in Russia. This journey has been a series of awakenings.'

'We are everywhere,' Ibrahim said. 'You are learning. Be warned that when you die, you discover it is a new beginning, but also that in the netherworld one becomes obsessed with one's past life. Yet not a single aspect of it can be altered: that is the tragedy of the afterlife. You are very privileged to know this before it is too late.'

'Are you saying I should make the most of it, then?'

'Indeed I am.'

'Indeed I will. Indeed it has already begun.'

'As for me,' Pushkin said, sitting up, 'I was married to one of the most beautiful, vain, fickle, empty-headed women in all of Russia, Natalia Ivanovna Goncharova. I think Oprah would say I was repeating the negative pattern of my relationship with my mother. One day I challenged her lover, a certain Baron D'Anthès, to a duel in an isolated spot near the Black River.

'It was the dead of winter. The ground was thick with snow. I was determined to kill him. He shot me first. I was carried back home. I was in the most horrendous pain. I lay on my bed. My body could not hold up. I had so many more books to write. I did not want to leave. I was fading in and out. My last words were "Life is ended. It is hard to breathe. Something is weighing me down."'

Pushkin lay on the cushion, and dissolved into it.

Outside could be heard the sound of noisy heels coming down the corridor. The Sultan wore slippers with silver soles to alert everyone that he was in the vicinity. The women stopped what they were doing and listened.

Ibrahim stood up, smoothed out his uniform and put an arm over Stanley's shoulder.

Stanley rose too. 'I don't want Pushkin to go. He was so full of, what's the word? Chutzpah. Can you ask him to come back? This is where I want to be. Going back to my real life is just too, well, complicated.'

'His time is up. When our time is up we have to leave. This is the unexpected nature of death. It is your time to go back too. To complete. Do not feel too sorry for him; he has more than enough self-pity. Perhaps that is why you two understood each other. In years to come your self-pity will make you an embittered old man. Be forewarned.

'As for my Alexander, he thoroughly enjoys replaying his death scene. When next we meet he will ask if it had the desired effect. In my heart he will always be the little boy who walked alone in the woods when his family summered at Zakharovo and my granddaughter was busy preening herself. I would walk beside him, willing him to sense my presence, but he did not possess the gift. He is probably dancing in the aisles of a James Brown concert now, or that other one he likes from Nigeria, that Fela Kuti fellow, who, Alexander tells me, sings in his underpants, accompanied by a chorus of women who lift their skirts and shake their ample, uncovered bottoms at the audience.' He paused. 'What *is* your world coming to?'

The heels stopped outside the room and a short woman entered in a smart blue skirt suit and stilettos, followed by a motley crew of tourists. She spoke in a clear, loud voice: 'Every aspect of the harem was exercised in accordance with ceremony and tradition. According to Islamic law, the Sultan was allowed four wives and . . .'

Life after the Camp Deserter

STAGE ONE: RAGE

Stabbing
(messy).

Drowning
(he's stronger than me).

Run him over so's he's flattened like a cardboard cut-out
(physically impossible).

Plant drugs, then shop him to Turkish police
(I might be implicated).

Sedate, smother in sleep, smuggle out to car, dump over cliff
(best yet, but he'll be too heavy).

Douse with petrol and set alight
(might arouse suspicion).

Poison, chop into manageable portions,
make mincemeat sausages,
preserve in deep-freeze of camp kitchen

and sell as hot dogs in Fethiye all winter
(most sensible, creative and profitable).

STAGE TWO: REGRET

The sun is running out of petrol.

Summer is speed-walking towards the horizon.
The drunken haze of heat is too soon sobered up.

Daylight is handing back its hours to darkness.
Wind is resurrecting the strokes of its cruel whiplash.

The lagoon is abandoned.
The camp has dismantled.

No more nightly gatherings.
No more *kum ba ya* singalongs.

I sleep with two single beds.
And nothing comes in the post.

(All the men I've loved and lost.
Oh, all the men I've loved and lost.)

These terrible departures.
These horrid ever-afters.

STAGE THREE: RECOVERY

Step 1 *Money*

Bought a Casio piano off a French boy at camp
whose parents were contemplating filicide

due to the hammering he were giving it.
Programme tunes / pretend to play. Easy.

Set up on the beach to catch the end-of-summer crowd.

Heaven, I'm in heaven, . . .

Step 2 *Support*

Dear Sunita decided to stay, loves passing
the saucepan around, badgering people to donate

to the fund for the 'struggling sisterhood'.
Says she can't leave me after the traumatic psychological
    torture

and sadistic emotional wounding that self-obsessed
male chauvinist trotter has put me through.

(Haven't the heart to tell her I've no 'inclinations'.)

Step 3 *Emotional Release*

Make enough for rent. Sunny helps out with food
and a few beers. We go to the Turkish Delights Disco

most nights and get plastered. Invented a dance
what looks like a mixture of kick-boxing, karate,

head-butting and fencing (without the swords).
It does the trick and keeps predators away.

(Won't touch a sou of his filthy lucre – till I have to.)

Step 4 *The Future*

Sunny wants to come on the road with us.
'Sure, we'll split the petrol and expenses.'

Won't Stanley mind? she asks, all considerate yet hopeful.
'Don't give a flying fuck if he minds.

I want you here, Sister Sunny.
Anyway, guess who's got the wheels?'

(My *bones* tell me he's coming back.)

STAGE FOUR: REVENGE

The Front Line

J Sunny and I were getting ready to go out. She'd disappeared into her tent to change into her disco outfit: a black bra showing underneath a baggy white string vest, a pair of ripped jeans, a pair of black, steel-toed Dr Martens and some war paint. I was quietly varnishing my fingernails green, when this *thing* enters the camp

S Whatever time has passed, whatever day it is, whatever time of day it is, whatever . . .

J His trainers are caked in what looks like shit, his jeans are filthy, his T-shirt stained, his face unkempt with bristle

S The campsite's nearly empty, and so – quiet

J There's nothing fearful or humble in his approach, just an air of . . . smug indifference

S How long *was* I gone? Ah, who cares. After all, time is more than the despotic hands of a clock telling me what to do and when

J 'Oh, hello, love,' I say, with a thick smearing of sarcasm. 'Had a nice time in Istanbul, dear?'

S And the high dive is still waiting for the bounce of my bare feet on its springy board. So long as Jessie is my safety net, I'll never really leap

J Oh, God! I've been painting my knuckles green!

S Yes, thanks. I had a really good time

J He says, as if he's just returned from a swim

S Do I have the courage to finish it? I don't know. In any case I'm going to fill her in. I have to tell the truth and face the truth. To complete?

J Why isn't he grovelling like last time? Damn! I've dripped nail polish on to my white disco trackies

S Jessie, we've not been on the same journey

J Here we go. Why does this always happen to me?

S Now hear me out. On the way to Istanbul I met a wonderful woman called Mrs Seacole, who was a nurse in the Crimean War. Once in Istanbul, or rather Constantinople, I hooked up with Pushkin and his Ethiopian great-grandad, who showed me around a harem. It was, well, it was like an out-of-body experience. This has been happening to me ever since we first met and, to be honest, I've loved every minute of it

J Stanley, that is the most pathetic excuse for cheating on a woman that was ever invented! Truth is, you went off with some young bimbo you met on one of your *long* expeditions to the toilet!

S I can see ghosts, Jessie. I've just been back in nineteenth-century Constantinople. It may sound crazy, but it's the truth. Listen to me. Hear me out. Just this once?

J You're trying to mess up my mind, you scheming little rat! You're insane, Stanley Orville Bastard Williams. And you've not even apologized!

S She loses it and starts frothing as insults fly out at falsetto operatic pitch and, I must say, with little regard for correct syntax. Like Ibrahim with the boy Menelik, I can see her, but I can't feel her any more. Maybe I am being a bastard. At least it makes me interesting

J Dear Sunny comes to the rescue

S That bitch shoots me her most disgusted of looks

Su What's happening, Jessie? He's being violent, isn't he? I'll call the police

S This is between Jessie and myself, so keep your nose out of it

Su No, it isn't. It's between the *three* of us now

S Oh, it's like that, is it?

Su Yes, it is. Come on, Jessie, we're going for a stiff drink. We need to get away from this prick-with-a-body-attached

J We storm off arm in arm. Me with green blotches of nail polish on my hands and clothes, and Sunny with one eye smudged with gothic-purple eye shadow that looks like a bruise

S Bull dykes

Güle, Güle, Ölüdeniz

S

throat

sword
levelled at my neck
for days

umbilical
throttles, can't scissor
yet

not bullfrog
stuck in oesophagus
but rhinoceros

Lucy, Louise-Marie, Joseph
Zaryab, Hannibal, Alessandro
Mary, Pushkin, Gannibal

J

throes

adieu, sweet Sunny
no Sapphic 'urges'
she skies to India

trees in the orchard
stripped of leaves
brittle

choppy/ cloudy/ cold
grey/ grimace/ grim/
git

penny drops:
some people will never, ever
ever-ever, never, ever-ever
change

S   J

whale music:
cries, howls, whistles
songs

                                    Walkman-crazed
                                    faraway glaze
                                    he's just gone 'off'

The Ocean Floor

. . . somewhere, out there, deep in the interminable ocean
a Blue Whale, a hundred feet long, follows its gravitational pull
you have returned to the waters where life began

I grab your tail, the wingspan of a small plane, you – monstrous,
    ocean-bound beast, largest of all creatures
that ever lived on my planet, spouting steam
as you cruise at twenty knots, your two hundred tons
of mammoth rage is mine
at last, we are sailing together, finally, Father

can you feel me diving through one of your man-sized blood
    vessels, while your stubborn pride soars on,
never able to settle, even though your chosen
country had changed, your home remained an island
in your childhood heart

well, this is your watery country now, Clasford, and say hello
to my new circle of acquaintances hereabouts,
a body of restless beings like yourself
because you will not release me

underneath the sea is the cold abyss
trenches a hundred miles wide into which you are falling
no daylight here, no photosynthesis in this underworld of gloom
an orange pea-shaped membrane eats you and becomes you,
shooting streaks of bioluminescent liquid into the black

there are fish with teeth so large their mouths won't close
others with eyes bigger than their bodies,
there are Firefly Squids here, Father
neon tips on their tentacles, bodies radiating with photophors,
like spangly lurex, but the pressure on my lungs
is too much and I am bursting with tears

as we sink seven miles down to the ocean's deepest trench, yet
here still, are pink coral polyps
pink coral polyps

your carcass lies, a long grey rock on the ocean bed, your chinless
wonder of a son is a scavenger at your flank,
a black slithery hagfish with no jaw,
wrapped like an eel into a knot to better extract your nutriments

this is where you belong now, this is home, embedded in clay
and fine oozes from sea creatures,
and when all your flesh is digested
I will suck all the energy from your bones
until I release you
I will take what is mine . . .

Eastern Anatolia

S We were driving towards our destination . . .

J First had to detour up to Ankara, didn't we, to apply for imposs-
ible-to-get visas. Told officials we were going for interviews as
teachers in Kuwait City (brainwave)

S Somehow, they bought it

J My mind is a powerhouse. My charm its tenants (not that it's
appreciated)

S Across the eastern fields of Turkey. Fewer towns. Fewer people.
Less friendly. No foreign number plates, except ours. 'Ours'?

J Spooky bloody place. Desolate. Raining. Not as spooky as *him* –
Whale Man. Adrift out the window

S I'm still here, aren't I?

J (In body) He's left me struggling to get a telephone connection
between my brain and my emotions. They're engaged but not to
each other

S I don't know how to spell it out to Jessie but – the line's gone
dead

J Eat kebabs in roadside caffs, mostly. Sleep in workmen's hostels
with no locks, no curtains, no sheets, no showers, no toilet paper,
but lots of detailed evidence of previous occupants

S We're 'hoping' there are boats from Kuwait to India rather than
Iran, Afghanistan, Pakistan . . .

J . . . because that writer Salman Rushdie has this fatwa against him
from the Ayatollah Khomeini, and what with all the diplomatic
souring it means Iran's off limits to us Brits. Ha, ha. That rhymes.
(Least something does)

S Now you care to mention it, Jessie, are we a rhyming couplet or a series of fake haikus? I mean, to be more explicit, are we a comma or a full stop?

J He turns to me, and, for the first time since he came back from his mind-screwing trip to Istanbul, a sixty-watt light bulb's switched on in his eyes. Why are you bringing this up in the middle of nowhere? Why does it have to be either/or? What about a hyphen or a semicolon? Chill out, will you?

S It may not be the most appropriate time to discuss this, but it's only because I didn't have the vocabulary before today. I had a rhinoceros lodged in my throat. Look, let's be honest with ourselves, Jessie. It's a full stop, isn't it?

J You wait until we're on our way to Iraq before throwing this at me! I know only two things, Stanley-Boy: your mental health is becoming a great big question mark and your personality is still nothing more than a blank sheet of A4 typing paper. Yes, I tried to splash it with some design and colour. Yes, I admit it, I failed, miserably

S Of course you're so perfect, aren't you, St Jessie? You know the answer to everything, while all I'm good for is benefiting from your vast experience. Your opinion is my opinion because I have none of my own. Well, you listen to this: I am so much more than your all-encompassing 'we'. And you, Jessie O'Donnell, as I have discovered, are not much more than a series of bold exclamation marks. To be blunt, to be really, really blunt, God knows what I'm still doing with you – because I, for one, do not

J Get out of my car, I growl, braking, pushing him out before he's aware that's what I'm doing. Then I drive off. Full stop. Exclamation mark (emboldened)

S It's pouring. We haven't seen another vehicle in hours. We're surrounded by wilderness. I storm off into it

J The switchboard's gone crazy, lines are crossed, everything's ring-ing at once, except the one call that can't get through. The one call that reassures me everything's going to be all right

S After a lifetime's worth of character-killing implosions, I finally lose it in the middle of a field surrounded by mountains. I start screaming, stamping the ground, fists clenched, eyes all screwed up and gummy, until my throat burns and I collapse on to the muddy ground, sobbing – for all the years and all the times I never could

J Must have gone half a mile. Turn round a bend, and wait

S I fling myself backwards on to the mud and lie there, sinking, arms and legs splayed. I let the earth take my weight and tears

J Five minutes. Ten minutes

S I want to close my eyes and sleep

J Twenty-five minutes. Now he's pushing it

S I need superhuman strength to scramble up and look for the car. My jeans are stuck to my legs, mud is plastered all over my hair, in my ears, under my fingernails. I'm clogged up with snot, and tears are starting to calcify on my cheeks

J There he is coming towards me, like an abominable creature lurching from side to side, slowly. Obviously hasn't learned his lesson, has he?

S I knew she wouldn't have gone far

J Switch on the engine as he approaches, then, when he gets close, scoot noisily off like some juvenile joy-rider. You started it. Happen I'll finish it, matey

S You mad heifer! I howl beneath the roar of engine and rain

J See him in the mirror, jumping up and down, punching the air, mouth opening and closing. Fifty yards down the road, I stop. Engine on. Let's see if you can eat humble pie now, Mr Quantitative Analysis

S I fight the impulse to start walking in the opposite direction. Night is sinking its claws into the fields and mountains

J Here he comes. What's this? Putting on that cocky amble of his what I hate. He reaches the door and *adios, amigo*, screeching tyres, full steam ahead, three hundred yards, at least. This is what happens when you turn your back on your guardian angel. This is what happens when you betray my trust, not once but twice

S I'm freezing. I'm sodden. I don't run towards her. I walk because, although Stanley is exhausted, Stanley still has his dignity

J Just as he reaches for the handle, off I go at full throttle. This is what happens when you break my little heart. This-is-what-happens-when-you-break-my-little-heart, *comprenez*?

S I don't care any more

J Fifteen minutes. Twenty. If only he'd stop playing silly buggers and run, he'd be sitting nice and cosy in Matilda's lap by now

S She's disappeared again. It's pitch black. No moon. No stars. It's too much. I want to curl up by the side of the road and go to sleep

J Thirty minutes and no sight of him in my back lights. Go into reverse. Where's the silly sod gone?

S I close my eyes and dream of the Friday evening I met a magnificent woman in a club called Mingles in Piccadilly Circus, London Town. How I drowned in her voluptuousness our first time together. How I discovered visitors from the past in that bed-sit in dingy old Clerkenwell. How I danced around a fire that first night in an empty woodland campsite in France. How she cooked a lovely meal for me on a little Calor gas stove. How we threw rosemary branches on to the flames. How we sipped Armagnac. How we gathered each other up in our eyes and held on tight

J Good Lord! Lying in a field like he's sleeping in a five-star hotel

S *Well, come on, gerrin, if you're coming*, startled me out of my reverie

J Well, come on, gerrin, if you're coming. I have to call out thrice before he wakes up and gets into Matilda, shivering. Bloody nutter

S She puts Nina Simone into the cassette deck and sings along:

There is a balm in Gilead
To make the wounded whole
There is a balm in Gilead
To heal the sin-sick soul

J Me, I'm a bomber and a sapper. Know how to detonate. Know how to diffuse

Slipping into the Middle East

Puddles of oil do not announce themselves but lie with the quiet patience of landmines, ready to skitter us into oblivion. We've finally picked up the main road to Iraq, and Jessie is forced to coax Matilda very slowly ahead. Yes, we have a sense of déjà vu, but at least it gets us talking again. A stream of oil tankers whizzes past us. Time is money on the oil run and the roadside is testament to the price. Tankers lie upturned on each side of it like garrotted skeletons with disembowelled bellies, which the wilderness of grass, bark and bracken has long since claimed as its own.

To our right is the barbed-wire fence of Syria. Behind us is the West. Inside me is a strange beast.

At the Zakho border I'm confined to a tiny room with fifty chain-smokers. Well, no, actually, oil tankers stretch back for miles, and every last one of them is pumping fumes, coating my face and lungs in a layer of grime. This is passive smoking on a murderous scale, I say to Jessie, who nods in agreement. Tea shacks and hawkers make the wait bearable. A driver, eager to practise his broken English with the real thing, tells us, somewhat furtively, that we're in a region known as Kurdistan, which spreads over from Turkey. We know little about the current politics of this part of the world. In this we are compatible, at least. We do know that the Iran–Iraq War ended over a year ago, which was also just about when I last read a newspaper. This from a man who used to read the paper religiously every day, and, if not, he'd get withdrawal symptoms. I recall there have been kidnappings in this area. If I ask, I might get confirmation, so I don't. Innocents abroad, or is it idiots?

It takes six insufferable hours to reach customs and immigration, and they give no more than a cursory glance at the eagle sticker in our passports, the *carnet de passage*, green card and other vehicle documents. Once we hit the motorway, the tankers divert off to oil fields.

We are on our own again, riding down the bumpy vertebra of

this long, narrow country. There's no time to visit the villages in the barely discernible distance. The landscape isn't the beautiful undulating sands of my golden imagining but a disappointing earthy-sandy substitute. Jessie can't drive fast enough to leave. I tell her it's not wise to put poor old Matilda through a heavy hammering. She ignores my advice. Nothing new there.

'All the road signs are in Arabic,' I exclaim.

'What did you expect? This is hardly Costa del Iraq. Baghdad is not exactly Benidorm and we'll not stumble across an Irish pub called O'Malley's in the desert.'

I remember what I like about her.

We park by a garage outside Baghdad for the night. Jessie's key in the ignition wakes me long before daylight. I wash with a cup of water and half a lemon. Survival training.

In the morning we drive around the outskirts of Baghdad and I'm just itching to visit the site of the famed Babylon of ancient Mesopotamia. Hey, I might bump into Nebuchadnezzar wandering around the Hanging Gardens, pruning roses and sipping mint tea. Wisely, I say not a word. At a set of traffic lights young men crowd the car, shouting for Jessie's hand in marriage. Are they really as sincere as they sound? So desperate?

'Marry my UK passport, more like,' she laughs. I laugh too. I cannot remember when last I did. We catch each other's eyes and smile. Hers contain hope yet.

There is only the never-ending road and my desire to get to the end of this particular one. We come to a fork near Basra. I say right. Jessie says left. She wins. (For a change.) We drive into what seems to be an old battlefield. Concrete lookout posts, derelict tanks, even the craters of military aircraft, just lying there, abandoned.

It is silent. It is creepy. Without saying a word, Jessie does a jumpy three-point turn.

'Whose idea was that?' she says, once we've left it behind.

'Yours,' I reply. I notice her hands are shaking on the wheel. Now *that's* a first.

'You're right,' she says. 'You see, I'm not afraid to admit when I'm in the wrong.'

As we approach Iraq's border with Kuwait at Safwan, I'm shocked to see it's occupied by a no man's land, people camped within its perimeter in makeshift tents, fenced off from both countries, perhaps for years. No way forward. No way back. For them, at least.

Night is getting ready to overtake us.

Here the border guards are more circumspect, spend some time studying our documents, poking about in the car, looking for contraband, such as alcohol. We stand to one side. Jessie has donned a headscarf that actually makes her look her age, or rather like a middle-aged housewife circa 1960. I'm tempted to tell her. Needless to say her cleavage hasn't been on show since we left Ankara. For the first time, she has to let me do the talking. *This is my fiancée, I am applying for a teaching position after a long sabbatical spent touring Europe and Turkey. How exciting to be visiting your wonderful country for the first time.* I do an excellent job of bullshitting. She, on the other hand, has affected a ridiculous hang-dog expression, accompanied by what can only be described as drippy sighs. I sidle up to tell her to ease up on the simpering. 'Bugger off! Know what I'm doing,' she mutters. 'As always,' I bat back.

Matilda is our sleeping chamber in the desert with two single beds. It's freezing, but our backs eye each other warily all night long. In the morning I get to see the amazing golden sands, and even the tail-end of a posse of wild camels disappearing over the dunes as if they've stepped out of a Lawrence of Arabia fantasy. Now that's one for a postcard. I'm looking forward to sending them again.

Kuwait City is introduced by functional tower blocks that I guess house the migrant workers who keep the wheels of this fabulously wealthy kingdom turning. Closer to the centre we encounter a vision of sun-struck marble houses that look like palaces. Coming out of the desert, out of Iraq, coming out of the eastern fields of Turkey, I find them surreal, untouchable, heavenly.

Jessie and I are grubby itinerants. Boy, must we stink.

Everyone drives brand-new Mercs, BMWs, limos. We stand out in the battered Lada Niva. I don't care. She has got us thus far and I feel quite attached to her. The car, that is.

We're starving. We're exhausted. We need a cool spring shower, but the sun is starting to spit and hiss and in the desert of all places a car needs air conditioning.

In the bazaar we discover a cup of coffee costs four times what it does in London. The chunkiest, gaudiest gold jewellery I've ever seen is hung in abundance inside shops. What looks like a simple kaftan costs four hundred dinar, and there are two pounds sterling to the Kuwaiti dinar.

'Let's hit the docks and get out of La-La Land,' Jessie says, shaking her head. 'Don't suppose there's much call for a cabaret bar here. Al-Jessah's Singing Bedouin Tent? I *don't* think so.'

There is no camping. No sleeping in the car. No amenities for tourists. No rooms for under a hundred dinar a night.

And.

There are no passenger ships to India – they stopped during the Iran–Iraq War.

One of us goes into shock and begins to cry. The other one suspected as much and is satisfied to have got this far overland.

A man might be able to find work on a ship, we are told.

My ears prick up.

Matilda is stamped into Jessie's passport. We already know that Jessie cannot legally leave any of these countries without her wheels.

I, on the other hand, have no vehicle stamped in my passport.

Once I've booked us into a suite at the Sheraton for one night (a hard-earned extravagance – how can she call me mean when she set out with four hundred pounds in travellers' cheques and she hasn't cashed a single one?), once we have showered and enjoyed what, after so long without, can only be described as a sumptuously exotic meal of cheeseburger and chips, coleslaw and ketchup, once we have settled down and she is zapping through the movie channel, I reveal my plans.

There never is a good time to hurt someone.

I will accompany Jessie back to western Turkey, where she will be safe driving alone. I will buy her a return ticket to Australia and give her money to survive for up to a year besides.

She is the one, I tell her, who brought me here and, in spite of everything, I am deeply grateful.

'The problem was never really about money, Jessie. The sad truth is that you and I *are* a knuckle and joint, but our groove simply does not fit.'

Her eyes fill up. 'You're snatching the magic carpet from under me, Stanley. I'm falling. I'm falling. Go on, be a love and catch me.'

'I can't.'

'Tell me what I've done wrong and I'll promise to correct it.'

'I don't know where to start.'

For the first time since we met, she is lost for words.

The next morning I hear her singing in the shower, '*No. No regrets. No . . .*'

The Supreme Court of 'Justice'

O'DONNELL v WILLIAMS

Jessie O'Donnell – *APPLICANT*
Stanley Orville Cleve Williams – *RESPONDENT*

The *APPLICANT* appeared in person and looked distraught

The *RESPONDENT* did not bloody bother to appear and was
not represented (my fault, like everything else, of course)

Before
LORD 'JUSTICE' THE ALMIGHTY

STATEMENT OF APPLICANT

I herewith present a *Skeleton Argument* in order to set the context
for my present predicament.

Did I commit *Adultery*? Did I commit *Bigamy*? Did I exhibit
Mental Disability? Was I the one guilty of *Unreasonable Behaviour*?
Was I the one guilty of *Desertion* two times without so much as a
Separation Petition?

Instead, was I not *Bona Fide* at all times, that is, true to myself
and therefore to him throughout the period of our *Cohabitation*?
Did I not pay due *Care and Attention* to the *Respondent* above the
call of duty, and also, did I not share my *Chattels*, namely my
caravan and my motor vehicle, Matilda, who, I might add, if she
were a person, could reveal much incriminating *Hearsay Evidence*
of said behaviour of *Respondent*? Actually, Matilda is *De Facto* the
Matrimonial Home in this case, which I did duly and fully and
willingly share with him.

Your Honour, hear my *Pleadings*, because, although he has

Secured Provision with *Lump Sum*, he has not undergone *Due Process*, that is, he has jumped to *Decree Absolute*, thereby conveniently and sneakily overlooking *Decree Nisi*. He has signed, sealed and delivered the *Terms* without *Negotiation* and thereby not allowed me the opportunity of a *Final Hearing*. Indeed, I am left out of *Service*. I am left *Undefended*. I am left with no *Relief*. I am left with only a *Prayer* that in the future I exercise *Proper Discretion* and not be taken in by a coward whose only method of coping with any minor *Conflicts of Interest* is to execute a *Clean Break*.

Oh, Lord, what have I done wrong this time! Why am I left alone again! I feel thoroughly *Annulled*. I feel of diminished *Valuation*, with no hope of *Reconciliation* and an *Overriding Objective* to pursue the inevitable *Course of Action*: to cry my heart out – until I am *Emotionally Bankrupt*.

Without prejudice
The *APPLICANT*

Antipodean Dreamtime

Surfs on Bondi Beach, Sundays, blue boxer shorts
(were always his favourite colour). Handsome fellow.

6 footer. 30 yrs. The wife, Gemma. No, ditch that. Melanie.
Nice girl, sits under an umbrella while the kid builds

sand castles. Lovely lad. Spitting image of Grandma.
His daddy owns a swish health club. No, ditch that.

He's an investment banker *and* a popular jazz singer.
Owns a sprawling white villa in Sydney with a garden

pink with bougainvillea (luxury guest cottage out back).
When Melanie asked about the iron-shaped indentation

burned deeply into his shoulder blade: *We were only kids*
larking about when this iron, set to Linen, set to Steam,

wasn't plugged out at all and my little mate Timothy
held on petrified for ages before he dared rip it off

with a layer of burned, melted cheese attached.
Left me allergic to ironing rest of my life. Ha. Ha.

Anyroad, he's striding up the beach, surfboard under arm.
No. He's playing footie with the boy, sees a familiar

gait approach. He peers. He cries out. He gathers up the boy
and starts to run, shouting out he can't believe I've come

after all this time, he can't believe I've come.

The Glorious Gulf

I'm standing on the crystallized shore of the Kuwaiti desert. The blistered fingers of seaweed are entangled in my grasping toes; the gasping inhalations of my chest are pulling me towards another life.

My black pupils are swollen bubbles. Two scouting swallows tear through the membrane and flutter off, dip into the curve of the Gulf, disappear over the Arabian Sea and towards the concave mass of the Indian Ocean. They are showing me. The earth's eternal centrifugal force is holding my world together. I can sense the submerged engine vibrating beneath my soles, making revolutions, yet I think I will fall off, or fly.

This is the plastic globe I once spun on my forefinger like a football, its geography reduced to minuscule printed nations, the countries I had to memorize, squiggles of borders I once carefully traced with a classroom compass: blue for water, green for forestry, gold for deserts. The meridians, zones, poles. What did it all mean to me then? That the world was 70 per cent water and floating continents, right? Another fact to ingest among the thousands of others called learning, from the breeze-block city called home, from where I took off, several lifetimes away.

And there, the equatorial line across my stomach, the fuse wire, the flaming roads behind me, each detonation has made me, the phantoms that came to me and turned my world around, the love that nearly consumed me, the death that I carried with me, the fires that forged me.

I feel like a monolith. I feel like a man now.

I have digested a small portion of the world and it has become me. Behind stand the modern, heat-shielding homes of Kuwait City, where the dismantled mountains of Egypt have been transported on to the oscillating sands of this roving kingdom. Their new foundations are bricks of black ingots. Behind is the city strung with pearls prised from the stubborn lips of deep-sea oysters by death-defying fishermen, who hunt for what they want in the subterranean depths.

Behind are the oil refineries of Iraq, the endless fields of Turkey and, further back, the vacillating topography of Europe: the A-roads, autoroutes, autostrada, the freeway that has led me here to this rasping beach, these waves littered with casually flung diamonds, this blow torch on my back, turning me a madder red and all else blazing glitter.

I cannot return home. Perhaps not ever. The mammoth ocean-going junks are anchored way off. They are waiting for me. Weighed down with the desert's siphoned blood supply. They know how to steer down the side of the world without falling off. If I do not go by sea, then I will fly thirty thousand feet above the earth, at six hundred miles per hour, and I will land, perhaps not on the moon, but I will be ready for it. I will be ready for anything.

And this is what I want.

Epilogue: Under the Carpet at Windsor

Queen Charlotte of England was desperate for some entertainment. She scratched her greater wing of sphenoid bone and yawned, breathlessly. It was so dreadfully dull lying prone in the chapel at Windsor, shorn of skin, with nothing sensible to do, for an eternity. Why be bored senseless when one could walk through walls and see what the latest new generation was getting up to? If only she could tell them to stop their constant complaining and get on with creating lots of interesting new experiences for themselves, because, when all was said and done, memories are all they will have to console them when they are dead.

Charlotte was still missing such basic earthly delights as riding side-saddle round the thousands of acres of Windsor Great Park, her dogs, her jewellery, the occasional soirée, her elephants that were housed in a paddock at Buckingham Palace, and O, how she had loved painting, playing the harpsichord, dancing 'The Hempdresser', reading books and going to the theatre.

Georgie was asleep as usual. He rarely woke up these days. It was such a tragedy that he should die blind, deaf and mad. (Although such a relief that at least he couldn't expose himself any more.) He had never got over joining the great unwashed of the netherworld, among whom he was afforded no special status whatsoever. At the end of his reign he once talked for fifty-three hours non-stop. Better he sleep, she mused, than that she should endure another round of his demented conversation.

'I am still appalled we lost America. Do you think we can get it back?'

'Oh, Georgie. You've still got a touch of the old madness yet.'

'Do we still have Ireland, Lottie darling?'

'Only some of it and only just. I personally believe we should hand it over.'

'Hush, woman! You know you are not allowed to meddle in politics. What about slavery? Do we have any? Anywhere in the world?'

'It was officially abolished during your reign. Do you not remember?'

'Remember? Remember? I remember when I first met you. I was smitten, not by your beauty, you were far too dusky for that (Ho! The courtiers called you all manner of things), but by your sweet disposition. Moreover, you gave me fifteen children. I still think twenty would have been a nice round number. Were they all mine, darling? Give me a kiss, my lovely.'

'Dislocated mandibles cracking against each other is very unbecoming, George.'

'If you say so. What about our granddaughter, Chubby Chops Victoria? Still mourning Albert? Playing the martyr? Hanging on to the throne for dear life?'

'As you well know, Victoria is with us down here, along with most of her nine children, who are always visiting and whom she cunningly married off into nearly all the royal houses of Europe. I like to think there's a little bit of me spread out all over the Continent.'

'Steady on, old girl. A little bit of me too.'

'We rather hope not, sweetheart.'

'So – who is running the show now?'

'Elizabeth, of course.'

'Good grief. She still at it? Four hundred years on the throne. Found herself a boyfriend yet?'

'No, darling, not Elizabeth the First. Elizabeth the Second. You know, little Lizbet – horses, corgis and foxes. *That* one. Married that Phil bloke who keeps putting his foot in his mouth.'

'I say, very unhygienic, what! Is she any good at the job?'

'Stable, respectable, iconic, stoic and dripping in obscene wealth.'

'Glad to hear we're still minted and the *people* haven't got their dirty little fingers on it yet. Any children?'

'Only four, which is quite the sensible thing. All alive and often misbehaving.'

'Am I alive, Lottie? Or have I kicked the bucket?'

'A long time ago, George. Now to sleep. You mustn't upset yourself.'

'Will you tuck me in?'

'Yes, dear. I will throw a few handfuls of dust on you if it will help you sleep.'

'Nightie, night, my darling.'

'Goodnight, dear.'

'God Save the King.'

'God help us all, George.'

The content of their conversations wavered, but never the tenor. What did they have to say to each other after two hundred and twenty-eight years of marriage?

Charlotte began to pace up and down the crypt, bristling with her favourite preoccupation. Where *did* she come from? It was always to George's credit that he did not show his disappointment when they first met in 1761. He had married her by proxy and unseen, after envoys had been dispatched across Europe and Princess Charlotte Sophia of Mecklenburg-Strelitz in Germany was chosen to marry King George III of England.

As soon as I arrived comments were passed on my swarthy complexion, the indelicate spreading of my nostrils and too-wide mouth, the frizz of my fair hair. Baron Stockmar, my personal physician, even dared to describe me as having a 'true mulatto face'. Surely it was not my descent from the Moorish line of the Portuguese royal house in the fifteenth century, as some are hypothesizing these days? Was I really one of those throwback creatures? Did not the reason lie closer to home? *Mutti? Papi?* Infidelities and embarrassments swept under the carpet, as usual? What about all those commissioned portraits, in which I look like either a snub-nosed pixie girl or an old West Indian washerwoman, depending on the painter? It was so embarrassing. Oh, dear, the very memory, but there's nothing to be done about it now. Georgie knew I had a kind heart, and that was all that mattered to him. I so wish that was all that mattered to me, but I am for ever compelled to ask myself the question, was my father indeed not my own?

Now, to that sorely needed distraction. Everyone is talking about this young man gallivanting about on the road who is wonderfully *susceptible*. Some are having the most tremendous fun with him. It is rare in the netherworld to be seen in one's original state – face, hair, body and dress – that we are all so very terribly excited. The last time we found someone *susceptible*, it was a three-year-old girl in Vladivostok some nine years ago. Naturally the conversation was a trifle limited.

Georgie will hardly miss me. He's sleeping soundly now and shan't wake up for another three years at least. I understand that this young chap is standing on a beach at the edge of one of those desert kingdoms and that he is feeling very passionate about life. This is just what I need. A young man, some passion and a sympathetic pair of ears. I had better realign my bones (they do go a bit skew-whiff with all my restless fidgeting) and hurry along out there before another wandering soul beats me to it.

Acknowledgements

Simon Prosser ★ Hannah Griffiths ★ Donna Poppy ★ Camilla
Hornby and all at Curtis Brown ★ Juliette Mitchell ★ Portia
St Hilaire ★ Jean-Claude Halley ★ Sebnem Toplu ★ Anni
Sumari ★ Sylvia Aiano ★ Luca Scarlini ★ Linda Le Merle ★
Maggie Gee ★ Jacob Ross ★ Nina Levine ★ John Mcleod ★
Suleika and Leila Rohd-Thomsen ★★ Jon Cook and the English
Department at the University of East Anglia for six months of
writing time when I was Writing Fellow in 2002 ★

BERNARDINE EVARISTO

THE EMPEROR'S BABE

Londinium, AD 211.

Meet Zuleika: sassy girl-about-town, hellraiser, the feisty and precocious daughter of Sudanese immigrants, now married off to a rich, fat, absent Roman and stranded in luxurious neglect. Until one day, that is, when the Emperor himself comes to town bringing with him not just love, but danger, too . . .

Dazzling, brilliant, streetwise, sassy, audacious, *The Emperor's Babe* has been hailed as one of the most original novels of recent years.

'Readable, sexy, delicious . . . I loved this book!' Helen Dunmore

'A glittering fiction whose words leap off the page into life. Brilliant'
The Times

'Youthful and daring, with hidden depths of wisdom and hilarity'
Independent

'Manages to move the reader from laughter towards tears. Unforgettable'

Daily Telegraph